12 BROWN BOYS

BY

MR. CREATIVE
OMAR TYREE

www.justusbooks.com

12 Brown Boys™
ISBN 13: 978-1-933491-12-7
ISBN 10: 1-933491-12-4

Text copyright © 2009 by Omar Tyree. All rights reserved. Published by Just Us Books, Inc. No part of this publication may be reproduced in whole or in part, or stored in a retrieval system, or transmitted in any form or by any means, electronic, mechanical, photocopying, recording, or otherwise, without written permission from the publisher. For information regarding permission, write to: Just Us Books, Inc., 356 Glenwood Ave., East Orange, New Jersey 07017.
www.justusbooks.com

Printed in Canada
12 11 10 9 8 7 6 5 4 3 2 1
Cataloging in Publication Data is available.

12 Brown Boys™ was created by Omar Tyree/Mr. Creative and is a trademark of Omar Tyree. All of the characters in this book are fictitious, and any resemblance to actual persons, living or dead, is purely coincidental.

Cover design and chapter graphics by Stephan J. Hudson, © 2009 by 2nd Chapter

CONTENTS

Chapter 1

Cool Dave

On Thursday, my English teacher Miss Travis told us to write a story about someone we admire. I hate it when she gives us homework. She's real pretty so I just wish we could come to class and stare at her.

Anyway, it's Sunday now, and I'm just sitting in my room at my desk. I don't know who I'm gonna write about, but my story is due on Tuesday. I was gonna write about Chuck D from Public Enemy. He's a rapper, and he has some real decent songs. I also like Heavy D, Rakim, and Ice Cube. But Miss Travis said that we had to write about someone we know personally. I don't know any rappers personally.

Man, this is taking all day, and I want to hurry up so I can watch the Dallas Cowboys beat the Washington Redskins on TV today.

"Michael," my father calls me. He pushes open my door and looks in. I look back at him and make a nervous smile, because I haven't written a thing on my paper yet.

"I need you to run to the store and buy a large bag of potato chips, pretzels and a 2-liter bottle of Pepsi soda," my father tells me. He takes out a $10 bill and puts it on my dresser next to the door. He closes my door and opens it again. "By the way, I mean now." So I put my winter jacket on and head to the corner store, two blocks away from our house.

I turn the corner to the store and spot "Cool Dave," walking from the opposite direction.

"Hey, youngbuck," he says to me. He reaches out his hand and I shake it.

Dave wears a leather 8-Ball jacket designed to look like a pool table. It has black, gold, green and red designs. And his blue jeans are tucked inside of his black Timberland boots. That's the style for the older guys in my neighborhood. So the old-head guys who live in my area of Oak Lane all look like mountain climbers or something.

"You gon' watch the Cowboys today, youngbuck'?" Dave asks me. He's smiling and looking all cool like he always does. Everybody calls Dave "cool." He *is* cool, too.

"Yeah, that's my team," I tell him. The Cowboys have Troy Aikman at quarterback, Michael Irvin at wide receiver, and Emmitt Smith at running back, and they are all good players.

Dave pushes open the corner store door before I can.

"You don't like the Eagles?" he asks me. The Philadelphia Eagles are our home team, but I still don't like them.

"Nope. The Eagles are sellouts and choke-sandwiches," I answer.

Dave laughs. "Don't worry, they'll get better," he tells me. He still likes the Eagles.

"Yo, Cool Dave! What's up, man? Where was you at last night?" this guy named J.C. asks him. J.C. is inside the store already.

"I was with my girl last night, man. You know how that gets. She wouldn't let me leave."

I start laughing after Dave says that. Man, he's cool. And a lot of girls like him because he keeps a haircut and a smooth face.

When I leave the store I start thinking, *I got it! I can write a story about Dave.* I know Cool Dave personally. He speaks to me and shakes my hand all the time. He's even a Cowboys fan. He likes Michael Jordan and the Chicago Bulls in basketball like me, too.

———

"HURRY UP WITH THEM CHIPS, MICHAEL!" my father yells up the basement steps as soon as he hears me close the front door. I run down into the basement with the bags of grub, thinking that a good football play is on, but it's only a Gatorade commercial.

"You better hurry up and finish that homework assignment before you miss all the good games today," my father tells me. He's wearing his extra-large Eagles shirt.

I go back upstairs to my room and start to think of what to write about Cool Dave. I remember when I first met Dave. It was four years ago, around 1987, when I was eight years old. I was hanging out on the playground. They even called him "Cool" back then. Dave's 18 now, so he must have been 14 at the time.

"Yo, Cool Dave! You down to play some football, man?" this old-head named Darnell asked him. It was a Saturday in September, and Dave was watching nine of us play from the benches.

"Naw, man. I'm about to go to the movies as soon as my boy, Tim, gets here," Dave said.

"Come on, man, just play until he gets here then," Darnell told him. He threw a pass at Dave. Dave caught the ball, flipped it around in his hands and threw it right back, real cool, like he was a pro.

"Aw'ight, but don't nobody get me dirty."

I guess Dave didn't want to mess up his brand new Nikes, his rust-colored jeans or his red Polo jacket. I wouldn't either. But anyway . . .

"Look, just throw me a bomb, D," he told Darnell. We were all inside of our huddle, and Dave came right into the game wanting a pass already.

"Aw'ight," Darnell said. I was kind of mad at that because I had only gotten one pass that whole game, and I had been playing football for almost an hour.

Dave ran straight down the field for a bomb and Darnell threw the ball like fifty yards, way up in the air, like a dark brown rainbow. Everybody stopped and watched while Dave ran as fast as he could with one man sticking him. Then he jumped up in the air and caught the ball. The guy who was sticking him fell down, and everybody laughed.

"Now, who can stick me out here?" Dave asked everyone.

He came right into the game and caught a touchdown. Man, he was cool.

"Aw, shut up, man. I slipped," the guy said. He got up off the grass and brushed the dirt off his clothes.

"Well, yo, I'll catch y'all later," Dave said. He threw the ball back to Darnell and started walking back toward the benches.

His friend Tim was walking from the basketball courts. "I saw you juice them boys," he said.

"Yeah, man, can't nobody stick me," Dave told him, shaking Tim's hand. From that day on, Dave was the coolest guy I know.

I sat and thought I'd write about that, but then I thought about another story that I could write about Dave. He was at the mall one time with a bunch of his friends, like two years ago. I was there shopping with my mom. These guys from West Philly were about to beat up Tim.

"Yo, man, it ain't even like that. He didn't know that you were talking to her," Dave was explaining to this short, stocky guy from West Philly.

"Naw, man, she told him. And he kept trying to talk to her anyway," the short guy said. They were arguing over a girl. The short guy was starting to take off his red Philadelphia Sixers jacket for a fight. At the time, my mom wasn't paying attention. She was deciding what store she wanted to shop in. But I continued to watch and listen to the commotion.

"Yo, Dave, I ain't scared of him, man," Tim said. Dave was standing in-between them, making sure they weren't close enough to throw any punches.

"What? Well, let's do it then, boy," the short guy said

taking his jacket off. There were girls all around them, being nosy. And a crowd of people started instigating.

"Tim 'bout to get beat up," this one girl said to her friends. They all wanted to see a fight. But then the mall's security guards came. That's when my mom started to pay attention.

She looked and shook her head. "Girls are always instigating something," she said. All I did was smile and continue to watch.

"What's the problem?" one of the security guards asked, stepping in front of the short guy and Dave.

"Man, I'm just trying to work things out with my man here, 'cause it was just a disagreement about whether my boy was trying to talk to his girl or not," Dave explained.

"Naw, it ain't no disagreement. I'm about to break this dude up," the short guy said, stepping toward Tim. The security guard snatched him by the arm. "What are you grabbing me for, man?" the guy complained.

"Because you don't live up here, and I've seen you before," the security guard answered. "You're always starting some kind of trouble."

"Ay, man, you better get off me. You don't know who you dealing with," the short guy said, struggling to free himself.

My mom and I continued to watch it all. She was just as curious as I was.

"Naw, man, it's cool. We were just talking things out, and all these people started crowding around, instigating," Dave said all cool and calm.

I couldn't believe it. He was speaking up and calling a truce. The security guard let the guy go, and Dave even shook his hand.

"It's cool, man. We got no static with you. My name is Dave."

The short guy calmed down and nodded his head. "Aw'ight, it's cool then, man. Just tell your boy to leave my girl alone."

"That's a bet. He'll do that," Dave told him.

That was s-o-o-o cool. Even my mom thought so. She smiled and said, "That was very mature of him. He worked everything out."

Then I remember this other time when Cool Dave picked me up in his black and gold Bronco Jeep. It was during summertime when I was walking back home from the barbershop.

"Hey, youngbuck. You headed back home?" he asked me. He leaned over his girlfriend from the wheel. She was sitting inside the passenger chair of his Jeep with earphones on, bobbing her head.

"Yeah," I told him. I liked those big, gold-trimmed sunglasses he had on, and his red Adidas sweat suit. Plus, his girlfriend had these big, circular gold earrings on that said "Nicole" across the middle. She was pretty, too, with a whole lot of hair in one of those Egyptian, statue-typed hairdos.

"Well, hop on in. I'm headed back your way now," he told me. His girlfriend leaned up in the front seat so I could squeeze in the back.

"You want some ice cream, youngbuck?" Dave asked me. There was an ice cream store on the way to the barbershop, but my parents had only given me enough to get my haircut.

"Yeah," I said.

"Aw'ight. Bet."

We pulled over to the ice cream store on the way back home, and we all climbed out of the Jeep to see what we wanted.

"Lord have mercy! Them curves get bigger every time I look at you, girl," Dave said to his girlfriend. We were walking inside the ice cream store, and Dave opened up the door so his girl could go in first.

"Would you stop saying that. I keep thinking that I'm getting fat," she responded to him.

"Yeah, fat in all the right places," Dave told her. And when she smiled, she had these big dimples on both sides of her face.

"What kind of ice cream you want, youngbuck?" Dave asked me. He took out this big roll of money and pulled out a $20 bill. He even had more money than my pop, seemed like.

"I want butter pecan," I said.

"Hmm, you like butter pecan, huh?" his girlfriend Nicole asked me. I guess that's what her name was. Why else would she wear big "Nicole" earrings if it wasn't?

Anyway, when I looked into her face, she started to look even prettier than Miss Travis. And Dave's girlfriend didn't wear glasses either.

"Yeah, I like butter pecan because my mom buys it all the time," I told her. I couldn't help smiling after that. Dave's girlfriend was making me feel real happy inside. She was giving me her personal attention.

"You gotta be home soon, don't you, youngbuck?" Dave asked me.

"Naw," I told him. I was lying, but I thought that he wouldn't know.

"Yes you do," he said. "You just trying to hang out. You think you slick." He and his girlfriend both looked at me and started laughing. So as soon as we finished ordering the ice cream, Dave started to drive me home.

He started singing to Nicole on the way. "I-i-i-i- d-u-u-u-u-u n-e-e-e-d y-u-u. I need y-u-u-u. I want y-u-u." It was Bell Biv Devoe's song, "I Do Need You." I liked that song. But Nicole started laughing again and told Dave that he couldn't sing. Then I started to wonder where the music was.

"You don't have a radio in this car?" I asked Dave.

"Naw, somebody stole my system last night. I think I know who did it, too. So I'm gonna get an alarm system hooked up before I get another one," he said.

When we finally made it back to my block, Dave let me out at the corner.

"All right, Mike, you stay cool, man."

I never heard him say my name much. He just called everybody who was younger than him a "youngbuck," and everybody who was older than him an "old-head." We all used those terms in Philadelphia.

Anyway, I didn't think about how Dave was able to buy his own Jeep at 18 years old until I heard these other guys talking about drug dealers at the playground one day.

"Now you know good and well that ain't no 16-year-olds got no money to buy no Cadillac. That youngbuck selling drugs, man, I'm telling you," one guy was saying.

"Naw, man, maybe his parents got money," the other guy argued.

"Well, if his family got that kind of money, they wouldn't even be living around here. I mean, this a nice neighborhood and all, but nobody got that kind of money around here to buy no 16-year-old a Caddy."

They weren't talking about Dave, but Dave's parents were not rich either. So where did he get the money from? I had never seen Dave work a day in my life.

Then I started seeing him and his friends hanging out on street corners for hours. And they were talking to lots of strangers who would walk by. One day I even asked him about it.

"What are you doing, Dave?" I asked him, before I had to go in. His left hand was shoved deep inside of his black and red sweat-suit jacket. He was wearing a black baseball hat pulled way down to his eyebrows. He looked nervous, too, like somebody was after him or something.

"Oh, what's up, youngbuck?" he asked me. He looked at me, overtop of me and around me. It was weird. Dave never acted weird before.

"Who are you looking for?" I asked him. I turned around to see if anyone was behind me, because he was acting like there was. But no one was there.

"Nothing," he told me. "But go on home, little man. I'm busy right now." He acted like he didn't want me near him.

I said, "Busy doing what?" He didn't look that busy to me. He was just standing around. Then he walked away from me. That was weird, too. Dave had never acted like that to me before. I shrugged it off and began to walk back home. But when I looked back and saw this dirty old man walk up to him, acting all shaky and stuff, I ducked down and hid behind a parked car to watch. I didn't want Dave to see me spying on him.

"Yo, I'll get with you later on," Dave told the old man who approached him. The man didn't even get a chance to say anything yet.

"You don't have nothing on you now?" the old man asked.

"I told you later on, man!" Dave yelled at him. He acted like he had an attitude. The man looked like he was about 45 years old, too. It's disrespectful to talk to your elders like that. My dad always told me to speak to your elders with respect no matter *how* bad they looked. Dad said that the "old-heads" would smack you in the mouth for being disrespectful when *he* was young. But if an "old-head" smacked a "youngbuck" in the mouth in my era, that "old-head" might end up in a serious fight.

The man told Dave, "I may not have it later."

Dave then looked in my direction to see if I was still there. He hadn't seen me duck behind the car. He turned back to the old man and said, "All right, give it here then," and took money from him. I waited to see if he would give the man drugs or anything, but he didn't. Instead, the dirty old man walked up the street from him and took something from under a rock. While Dave watched him carefully, the man shoved something inside of his pants.

When the man walked away, I started to wonder what was under the rock.

Probably drugs, I told myself. I was curious and wanted to sneak up and look under the rock to see it for myself. But I didn't. It might have been dangerous. Dave had already told me to leave. But I stayed behind the car and watched. A skinny lady walked up to him next. Dave looked around again to make sure that no one was watching him. The skinny lady gave him money, too. She had it balled all up in her hand. Then she walked across the street to get her drugs from the under the rock.

That was all I needed to see. They weren't giving Dave money for nothing, and it wasn't food or drinks under that rock. So, what else could he be selling to them?

I don't know if Dave saw my head pop up from the behind the car or not, but he suddenly walked around the car where I hid and caught me trying to sneak away.

"Yo, ain't your pop looking for you?" he barked at me. He sounded mad. He said, "You better get back to the crib before he come out here and embarrass you again for hanging out too late."

Dave was trying to get rid of me by bringing up bad memories. But I had already caught him selling drugs. I was thinking, *at least I'm not a drug dealer, sneaking around on corners, selling drugs to dirty old men and skinny women.* But I didn't want to say that in front of Dave. My heart was already racing fast from him catching me spying. And maybe Dave would have tried to hurt me for doing that. So I got a move on without saying a word. My heart was still pounding fast in my chest when I made it back home.

———

Man, I don't know if my parents would like me writing a story about Dave if he's a drug dealer, I started thinking to myself at my desk in my room. Even though Dave had tried to keep it away from me, selling drugs was wrong. And I could never forget about him doing it. I couldn't bring myself to write a good story about him. Dave was making bad choices, and that *wasn't* "cool".

I start to think about writing a story about my dad instead. My dad works real hard, he protects our house, and he fixes a lot of things that are broken. He cooks and barbecues whenever we have family picnics or holidays, and he can lift our big air conditioner all by himself. My pop is even funny sometimes.

So I decide to write a story about my dad, and when he reads it aloud he laughs. He says it is good, too. Then he tells me that I have to write it over because I have too many mistakes in it. But he does let me watch the Cowboys beat the Redskins before I write it over though. He lets me watch the football highlights on the ESPN sports channel with him, too. And while I am watching the highlights on TV in the basement and listening to my dad argue with his friends about what team would go to the Superbowl, we hear all these police sirens outside.

"What in the world is going on?" my father says. We all go out the back door and walk around the corner of our block. There are like ten cop cars in the middle of the street.

"What is happening out here?" my father asks one of the neighbors.

"It was a shoot-out, with those crazy, young drug dealers," this lady answers.

All of a sudden, my heart starts beating real fast. What

if it was Cool Dave? What if he has been shot by a rival drug dealer, or somebody trying to steal his drugs and money? And what if he is dead?

"Do they know who it is?" I ask the lady.

"Yeah, they know who it is. It was them boys that hang out on Ogontz Avenue," the lady says. Dave didn't hang out on Ogontz Avenue. He always hangs out near the playground.

When I start to walk back home with my dad, I begin to think about Dave again. I am worried about him because the "Stop The Violence" video, by the rappers in New York, said that 84% of young Black men are being killed by other young Black men. Even the rappers in California made a video, "We're All In The Same Gang" to stop Crips and Bloods from shooting each other over turf wars and revenge in Los Angeles and Compton.

Man. I still like Cool Dave. So I pray, *Please don't let anything happen to him, God. He's only 18 years old. He don't even have a house and a family yet.*

Maybe Miss Travis will give us another assignment to write about people who we would like to change. Because I would write that story about Cool Dave. And then, if I could have it my way, I would make Dave my older brother. He's not like, a monster or anything. He just needs somebody to help him learn how to get paid in another way, and to make better decisions in his life. He needs somebody like my dad. And that would be *real* "cool."

Chapter 2

RED-HEAD MIKE

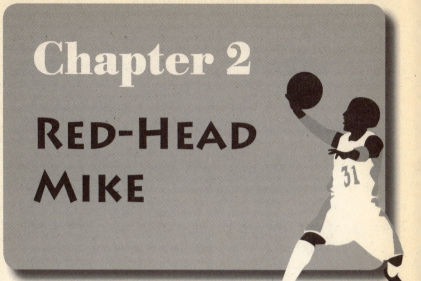

"Hey, Red-Head Mike, what's happenin', shorty?"

Michael McDaniels turned and shook the older boy's hand. "I'm doing good," he responded. But he hated being called by that nickname. His schoolmates had started a neighborhood trend that had stuck with him for the past four years. Imagine having bright, reddish brown, curly hair with golden brown eyes and skin. With that striking color combination, Michael stood out like a high wattage light bulb everywhere he went. Ever since he had entered grade school, he was forced to answer to his torturous nickname. He had even tried to keep his hair cut low for a whole year, hoping that people would forget about its bright red color. Unfortunately, Michael had reddish brown eyebrows and tiny, skin hairs that were noticeable on his arms and legs to remind everyone of his unusual hue. When he finally let his reddish-brown curls grow long on his head again, he decided to deal with whatever people would call him.

"Where you on your way to?" the older boy asked him. He was a young teenager, long legged and energized. Mike, one year away from his own teen years, was relaxed and mature beyond his age. People said he had an old soul.

"I'm on the way to the corner store for my grandma," he answered.

"How she doin'? Everything all right?"

Michael nodded. "Yeah, she's good. Thanks for asking."

"All right, be cool then, dawg," the teenager told him.

Mike nodded and continued on his way to the corner store in his southwest Houston neighborhood. He didn't notice the two giddy girls who were watching him from a distance.

"Oh, my God! There go Red-Head Mike," the girls reacted excitedly. But Mike was focused on his errand.

When he walked into the store, Mr. Hinton, who had owned the neighborhood grocery shop for the past 35 years, greeted him like everyone else did.

"Hey, Red-Head Mike, what's shakin'?" he asked in his scratchy southern drawl. Mr. Hinton was a gray-haired man who wore large reading glasses. He was more than 70 years old, but he never told anyone his exact age. Instead, he turned all of the old age conversations into jokes.

"My grandma needs milk and eggs to bake her strawberry cake," Mike answered. Then he gathered a dozen large eggs and a quart of whole milk.

Mr. Hinton chuckled. "She still got that sweet tooth, huh? You betta' tell her they gon' fall out, she keep baking all these cakes."

Mike laughed and said, "I tell her that all the time, but she don't listen to me. She say that sweets are good for your heart."

Mr. Hinton heard that and grinned. "You can say that again. Sweets make a man smile."

When Mike placed the milk and eggs on the front counter to pay for them, the same two girls from outside walked in and bumped into each other at the doorway.

"Watch where you walking," one said to the other. She seemed to be the leader of the two, with more confidence.

Mike pulled out a $10 bill from his pocket to pay for the milk and eggs. And even though he ignored the two girls, they still walked up to him.

"Hi, Red-Head Mike," the lead girl greeted him.

Mike smiled, showing them courtesy, just like his grandmother had taught him. "Hi," he answered.

Mr. Hinton bagged up Mike's groceries. He looked over at the two young girls and cracked another grin. He asked them, "You girls in here to buy some candy, or you just lookin' today?"

The lead girl spoke up again. She had a short ponytail and was slightly taller and browner than her friend. She was even an inch or so taller than Mike.

"Umm, we're just lookin' around," she answered Mr. Hinton.

Mr. Hinton looked directly at Mike and said, "Yeah, I see ya' lookin'."

Mike continued to ignore it all. It just seemed to him that everyone liked to stare and call out his name for no good reason. He didn't even know the two girls. He remembered seeing them around the neighborhood a few times, but they were not friends of his. He gathered his change and the two separate bags of eggs and milk and headed home.

As soon as Mike walked out of the store, a group of three teenage boys were just about to walk in. They were all wearing athletic shorts and tops, and they were tossing a basketball back and forth between them.

"Hey, Red-Head Mike. What's up?" they all greeted him. Since they couldn't shake his groceries-toting hand, they knocked elbows with him instead.

"Y'all 'bout to run ball?" Mike asked them.

"Yup. You wanna get a run with us after you take them bags home? We headin' over to the rec center after we buy something to drink."

As the teenage boys spoke to him, the two giddy girls walked back out the store, empty handed.

One of the guys then grabbed the lead girl around the waist.

"Hey, Bernadette, when you gon' be my girlfriend? You ready yet?"

Bernadette pushed him away and snapped, "Never," she said, "I already told you, Courtney, I don't like you like that."

Courtney looked the girl in her face and was surprised by her overreaction. She seemed to be putting on a show.

She never reacted that strongly to him before. Courtney always joked with Bernadette about her being old enough for a boyfriend.

"You never told me nothin' like that. I always joke with you," he reminded her.

"Well, she tellin' you now," one of his friends commented with a laugh.

"When I'm ready for my first boyfriend, I'll be sure to let whoever he is know," Bernadette announced loud enough for them all of to hear.

"I heard that," another one of the teen boys responded.

Mike was still standing there taking everything in. Then it dawned on him that he had to take his grandmother's groceries home.

"All right, well, I'll see if I can catch up to y'all at the rec center," he told the older guys.

"Yeah, you do that, dawg," they responded. "We'll be there."

Bernadette overheard Mike talking about going to the rec center and decided to ask him about it. "Is that where you're going?" She waited patiently for his answer.

Mike looked at the girl and thought about her question. He figured she didn't know him well enough to ask him how he planned to spend his free time. So he didn't know how to answer her.

Courtney looked at the sparkle in Bernadette's eyes, and then looked back at Mike. He said, "Oh, now I get it. So you like my boy, Red-Head Mike, huh?" She was sure giving him all of her attention, and Courtney was reading between the lines.

Bernadette's girlfriend started giggling uncontrollably as soon as Courtney asked the question. She figured her girlfriend had been busted.

But Bernadette surprised them all when she answered, "Maybe I do."

Mike was shocked by it. What was he supposed to say to that? Instead of responding, he shook his head and started walking toward home again.

Courtney stopped him and said, "Mike, she said she likes you. What are you gonna do about it?"

Mike was still thinking about getting the groceries home to his grandmother. He said, "I heard her."

"Well?" everyone asked. They all wanted to know what his response would be. All eyes were on Red-Head Mike, once again. And he didn't really like all of that attention.

He shrugged his shoulders and said, "I don't know. I just gotta get these bags back to my grandmom."

"Aw, man, you betta' act like you know what time it is with this girl," the guys responded. "She just said she likes you."

Bernadette didn't like them changing her words. She argued, "No I *didn't*. I said, *maybe*."

Well, Mike didn't have any time for the he say, she say arguments. The milk and eggs would get hot. That was his cue to get moving again. "All right, I'll just see y'all at the rec center after I take this home."

They were all disappointed in Mike's lack of response to them, but what could they do about it? He wasn't interested.

As Mike walked back home, a few people cruising by in a car screamed out his nickname.

"Red-Head Mike, what's poppin', player?"

He didn't even see who it was in the car, a light blue Chevrolet. He raised the bag of eggs in his right hand and waved it at them as the car zoomed by and headed up the road.

Even a group of preschool kids, who were playing inside of a locked gate at the daycare center stopped to stare at him. Mike had to pass them on his way home.

"Look at his hair," one kid commented, pointing.

The kids were wide-eyed and staring. "Wow," they responded.

Mike shook his head and grumbled to himself, "I should have worn my baseball hat." In his rush to make it to the store and back, he had forgotten to wear it. And by the time he made it back home to his grandmother with her groceries, Mike had heard enough about his hair to last an entire week. He felt like burning it all off so for once he could walk down the street in peace. The same went for his eyebrows.

While his grandmother started on her strawberry cake inside the kitchen, Mike sat outside on the patio in front of the back lawn, where few neighbors could see him pouting.

"I hate this hair," he mumbled under his breath. He then shoved his Houston Astros baseball cap on his head. He didn't feel like going to the rec center anymore. All it would do was draw more attention to himself.

A few minutes later, his Uncle Raymond walked into the house. Mike could hear him inside the kitchen kissing his grandmother on the cheek.

"Hey, Mom, you bakin' another cake again, huh? What kind is this one?"

"Strawberry," she told him.

"Strawberry? Now you know my favorite is lemon."

"Well, you're not the only one eating them, Ray," she told him. "I can't bake cakes only for you."

"Yeah, I know, I know," he responded. Then he walked outside to the back and spotted his nephew, looking all gloomy with his face in his hands.

"Hey Red, what's going on with you today? How come you're not out at the park or the rec center somewhere?"

Mike turned to face his uncle and snapped, "Stop calling me that." He had an angry look on his face.

His Uncle Raymond looked at him and frowned. "Stop calling you that? I always call you Red."

Mike said, "Well, I don't like it. I hate people calling me that. They do it all the time."

His uncle couldn't help himself. He started laughing and said, "What, Red-Head Mike? You hate people calling you that?"

Mike looked up at his uncle with pain in his eyes. "Yes," he answered.

At that point, Uncle Raymond understood how serious it was. He took a seat on the patio next to his nephew to explain a few things. "Michael, he said, "let me tell you something. Do you know how many people in this world have your name? It's gotta be at least a million of them. You got Michael Jordan, Michael Jackson, Mike Tyson, Michael Johnson, Mike Epps, Michael Williams and the list goes on and on and on. But when people call you 'Red-Head' Mike, you stand out."

"But I don't like it," Mike repeated. "I didn't choose to have this hair. I was just born with it."

Uncle Raymond started to chuckle again. He had light-brown skin, lighter than his nephew's, but his hair was a dark brown.

His nephew told him, "People don't talk about *your* hair all the time."

"I wish they did," Uncle Raymond said. "You know how many people talk about you? Everywhere I go, they ask me, 'Hey, man, how's your nephew doing?'"

Mike blew it off and said, "They're just being nice."

"So what?" Uncle Raymond told him. "They're still asking about you. They don't have to be nice. And they don't ask about everybody. So it's a good thing when people ask about you."

Mike didn't seem to care, so his uncle continued with a smile. "And the girls, they talk about you, too. 'You Red-Head Mike's uncle, aren't you?'"

He looked at his nephew. "Boy, you got me in more conversations with these mommies than I ever could by myself. I remember I used to take you with me everywhere I went just to get that attention.

"'Is that your son?'" his uncle mocked in a woman's voice. "Naw, this here is my nephew. 'Well he's cute.' And then I'd go right ahead and get their phone numbers."

After that comment, Mike started grinning himself. His Uncle Raymond had always been a great storyteller.

"So you were using me just to get women," Mike said.

"Well, you can use yourself now," his uncle told him. "You're old enough. And people like you. You don't realize that?"

Mike argued. "They don't like *me*, they just like talking about me because of my hair."

"Who cares why they talk about you as long as they're saying good things?" Uncle Raymond reasoned. "Do you understand that famous people hire publicists to keep their names and faces popular? People actually pay for that. But all you have to do is walk into the room and take your hat off. Boy, do you know how powerful that is?"

His uncle couldn't believe that Mike was actually pouting about the situation.

"I just want to be left alone sometimes," Mike admitted. "I just want to look normal."

Uncle Raymond shook his head. He stopped and said, "Yeah, I know what this is. You're still young. That's all. And a lot of times young people don't understand how to use a good thing when they got it. It happens to all of us."

"But if I was you . . ." He stopped and shook his head again. "Look, boy, if you don't want it, then let me take your curly red hair and your looks right now. I'll show you what to do with it."

Uncle Raymond took off Mike's hat and tried to pull his hair out of his head. This got his nephew laughing.

"Ouch, that hurts," he winced.

"Exactly," his uncle said. "It hurts me to hear you complaining about being special. Every kid out here wants to have something that people notice them for. That just happens to be your hair right now. But you can use that popularity to your advantage. That's what you do with it. Don't complain about it."

Mike was silent for a minute. His uncle continued to explain.

"I bet that right now you could walk around the corner to the rec center, and every kid in there will want to talk to you or be around you. The little girls too," he told him. "But there's other kids in there who they never pay attention to, for anything. And you need to think about that before you start complaining about all the attention that *you* get. You're just popular, Red. Learn to live with it."

That was all his Uncle Raymond had left to say. He stood back up and walked into the house.

Mike sat there for another minute by himself and thought about the game of basketball that he was missing out on at the rec center. Why should he punish himself just because people took a wild and crazy interest in the color and texture of his hair? He took a deep breath and stood up, and planned to go and enjoy himself with his friends.

"Hey, Grandma, I'm going around to the rec center," he said.

"Okay, and you be safe on the way there," his grandmother replied. "And make sure you be back home in time for dinner."

"Okay," Mike told her, and he was out the door. Mike walked down the street toward the Southwest Houston Recreational Center with pep in his step. He got so excited about his uncle's explanation about the popularity of his hair, that he started running to get there. But, he still wore his Astros hat over his head.

When he arrived at the rec center, Mike paused to catch his breath before he entered the massive, three-year-old, red brick building.

Here I go, he thought to himself. Mike walked inside the building and headed straight for the basketball court. Then he looked around to spot his older friends. Luckily, they were just starting to choose their team for the next game.

Courtney saw Mike and shouted, "Hey Red-Head Mike, you still running with us?" He said it loud enough for everyone inside the gym to hear. And they all started to look again.

Mike expected the attention now. He smiled, took off his hat and tossed it on the benches. "Yeah, I'm still playing."

As he jogged to the basketball court, a group of young girls were practicing their cheerleader moves near the sideline, including Bernadette and her friend. They were all smiles again as soon as Mike walked by them. Mike stopped and spoke to them all.

"Are y'all cheering for me, or for everybody?" he asked the girls with a grin.

They couldn't believe he was speaking to them. Red-Head Mike usually only spoke to people after they had spoken to him first. All the girls lost their cool.

"Oh, my God, we'll cheer for you," they responded excited.

"Thanks, I need it. I can't play basketball that good."

But the girls didn't care. They were just happy that Mike spoke to them.

I guess my uncle was right, Mike told himself. *I'm real popular.*

As he entered the game, Courtney noticed all of the attention Mike was getting inside the gym, and he had to warn himself, "Don't let it go to your head, man. Because if they're all cheering you now, then they can see how bad you are when you miss."

Mike took that warning and flipped it around. He said, "But if I play good, then they'll all know how good I am."

Courtney heard him and grinned. He said, "Okay, we'll see. But just remember that you asked for it."

Red-Head Mike smiled again, thinking about his uncle's advice. *If you have something that works to your advantage, then learn to use it.* And that's just what he planned to do.

Chapter 3

READING CLASS

Antwan Worthy, a fourth grader at Phillis Wheatley Elementary School in Northeast Washington, DC, sat at his wooden desk near the front of the classroom on Monday afternoon. He stared down at his empty desktop and was so nervous that he felt sick to his stomach. He folded and then unfolded his hands on the desk. He played aimlessly with his sharpened pencil. And under his desk, he bounced his right leg up and down like a hummingbird in steady motion. He knew that at any moment, Miss Palmer, his reading teacher, would call him up to stand at the front of the class to read aloud from a book.

The problem was, Antwan hated to read, especially aloud in front of his classmates. What if he made a bunch of mistakes? He never considered himself to be a good reader anyway. So why was Miss Palmer ready to torture him? Didn't she realize that everyone did not feel comfortable reading in front of an entire classroom?

"That was a very good job, Tabitha. You may take your seat now," Miss Palmer said to Tabitha Brown. Tabitha had just read aloud from a Judy Blume book. She was so pleased with herself that she returned to her desk with a smile on her face and a skip in her walk.

So what? Antwan thought to himself as he watched Tabitha skip down the aisle to her seat. Her desk sat directly behind his. *Girls just like to read,* he thought. *But I like math, science and gym.*

Nevertheless, Miss Palmer called him to read next, just like he knew she would. She had told him to pick out a book over the weekend. Although Antwan had been able to select a book of his choice, he still was not eager to read it. Picking out his own book to read was like picking his own nasty medicine to slurp from a spoon. He kept the book inside of his desk, hoping that Miss Palmer would think that he left the book at home and skip him. Or maybe he would lie about it and say that he forgot his book and left it at home by accident. Or maybe he would say he lost it. Or maybe . . .

"Antwan Worthy, would you please come up front to read from your book?"

It was too late. Miss Palmer had called him to his death. Antwan looked at her with wide eyes, praying that she would allow him a second chance to live and not step forward to read. But it was no use. Miss Palmer looked toward the spot at the front of the classroom where he was to stand and read without making further eye contact with him.

Antwan took a deep breath and reached into his desk to pull out his selected book, *The Werewolf of PS 40*, a *Kid Caramel* story. It was book number two in a series about a young brown boy who solved mysteries as a private investigator with his sidekick "Earnie."

Antwan sure took his time to walk up front. It looked as if the small paperback book weighed a ton in his right hand. He carried it limply at his side as he shuffled forward.

"Come on, Antwan, we all know you can walk much faster than that. Just treat it like it's gym class," Miss Palmer told him.

But it's not gym class, Antwan thought in a panic. *It's a book reading!*

Once he stood in front of his peers beside Miss Palmer's large wooden desk and turned to face them, Antwan immediately spotted the other boys who were all ready to snicker and tease him. Or at least it seemed that most of them were ready to do so. They understood his shame and terror. It was only normal for the guys to feel that way about reading. The only boys who read well were the geeks and nerds of the classroom; the sissy boys. Or at least that's what Antwan and his gang of athletic guys thought.

"You may begin now," Miss Palmer told him.

Antwan stood in front of the class and daydreamed about being somewhere else. Anywhere! But Miss Palmer was not going to allow it.

"We're still waiting," she told him.

Antwan fumbled with the book in his brown hands and uttered, "Umm . . ."

"Ha ha ha," a few of the other boys began to laugh.

"Silence, or I'm taking away your recess," Miss Palmer warned them with a pointed finger.

That didn't make Antwan feel any better about it. So what if she punished his classmates? He still had to read to them. So he cleared his throat and looked down at the open book to begin on page one.

"It . . . was . . . the . . . first . . . day . . . of sci, sci, school," Antwan stuttered after beginning slowly.

"He he he," the boys began to giggle.

"Samuel, no recess," Miss Palmer scolded immediately, catching one of the silly classmates in the act.

Samuel raised his open palms with a face of shock and confusion. "What did I do?" he asked her. His eyes stretched wide with innocence. But it didn't work.

Miss Palmer pointed her finger at him and said, "You already know what you did. And it's not easy for anyone to stand in front of the room and read. But you're all going to do it *several times* before this year is over, and before you move on to the fifth grade. I can promise that to everyone in this classroom."

A few of the boys looked at Miss Palmer's small, chocolate brown frame while she sat behind her desk, and they were ready to challenge her authority.

"But why do we all have to do that?" Bobby asked from the back of the room. He was big and bold enough to ask Miss Palmer that question for all of the boys. It was obvious to them all, that on average, the girls were the better readers.

Antwan spoke up in agreement with Bobby. He turned to face Miss Palmer at her desk and said, "Yeah. Why do we all have to read in front of the class?"

Couldn't she see that the boys would continue to laugh at each other whether they lost their recesses or not? They just couldn't help themselves. Other boys in the class had lost their recess every week during their reading periods.

Miss Palmer told them, "Because you all need to learn how *not* to fear reading aloud or speaking intelligently in public. You have to learn to *read* and *speak* with confidence."

"But we can read to ourselves like we do in private reading time," Samuel suggested. "No one wants to hear a kid read out loud."

Miss Palmer smiled at Samuel. Then she turned her smile to face every other student in the room. She asked them all, "Are you sure about that? I, personally, love to hear kids read aloud."

"Well, that's *you*," Bobby stated boldly from the back of the class again.

Miss Palmer kept her composure and said, "A kid who can read well aloud is a well respected kid. Don't you guys respect Ludacris, T.I. and Lil' Wayne? They're all speaking out loud," she alluded to three urban rap stars.

"Yeah, but they're not reading," Antwan disagreed. "They already memorized that stuff."

Miss Palmer smiled at him and responded, "Well, why don't you memorize your reading then? That would be more impressive than holding the book out in front of you. That would make you a prepared stage performer."

Samuel looked infuriated by the idea. "Rappers aren't memorizing stuff from books," he said. "A lot of them know how to freestyle. They make it all up on the spot."

"Well, we are not *free*-styling in my classroom. In my

classroom we're all going to learn how to read, *and* how to read in front of others, and with material that you may have never seen before," Miss Palmer told them.

As more of the fourth grade students began to bicker, including a few of the girls who didn't care much for reading in public either, Antwan looked at Miss Palmer and was still confused.

"Well, if we can't see it before we read, then how can we memorize it?" he asked her.

"That's my point," she answered. "A lot of the things that you'll have to read in your lifetimes, you won't have a chance to memorize. You'll be forced to read something new and then answer questions about it right there on the spot, just like you do now with your end of year exams."

"But they only do that in school," Bobby stated.

Miss Palmer responded with a smile. "Well, if Antwan Worthy runs out of time to read his book to us before the bell rings, because *some of us* want to argue about the importance of *reading*, then I guess we'll *all* stay in for recess until he finishes."

That response sent the entire class into an uproar.

"What? Why do we have to stay in for recess because of them?" an angry girl protested.

"Yeah, that's not fair to us," Tabitha agreed with her.

"All because they don't like to read," another girl spoke out. "We don't get to sit out during gym class. We have to do everything that they do."

"I know."

The girls were all up in arms about it. Antwan took it all

in as he continued to stand at the front of the class with his book in hand. He didn't want everyone losing their recess on account of him either. It was unfair to all of them.

Antwan took a deep breath and looked back to Miss Palmer who was standing behind her desk. He said, "I'll stay in for recess by myself then. They shouldn't have to stay in because of me. I'll just read it by myself."

Antwan was willing to give up his recess for the benefit of his classmates, but at the same time, he knew that would get him out of reading in front of them. He figured that the punishment of reading aloud was three times worse than giving up his recess. At least the loss of recess would only be for one day. Classmates teasing him about his bad reading skills could go on forever.

Miss Palmer nodded to him and said "Well, that's very nice of you, Antwan, to sacrifice for your fellow classmates that way. But if I allowed you not to read to them, that would defeat the whole purpose of this exercise."

Aw, man, I hate her guts! Antwan thought to himself. Not only was Miss Palmer mean, she was mean with a smile on her face. That seemed to make her meanness more unbearable.

She said, "But I'll tell you what, if you can continue reading to us at your own comfortable pace, then I can see where you leave off and we'll pick back up from that spot tomorrow.

Antwan didn't like the sound of that idea either. A continuation of his reading meant that not only would he be embarrassed for the rest of that day, but he would have to start all over again a second day. But his classmates liked the idea as a compromise. They would still have their recess.

"Yeah, let him finish reading it tomorrow then," the majority of his classmates agreed.

Antwan took another deep breath, and picked back up reading from *Kid Caramel*'s first chapter.

"Act, act . . ."

"Sound out the word," Miss Palmer interrupted him.

Antwan listened and stated, "Act-u-ually . . . it . . . was . . . more . . . of . . ."

RIIIIIIINNG!

The bell rang to end class before he could finish his sentence. Antwan's classmates hurried out into the hallways before Miss Palmer could change her mind about recess.

Whew! Antwan thought to himself. *It's finally over. But now I have to do it all over again tomorrow.*

"Antwan, let me speak to you a minute," Miss Palmer said as she stood up from her desk. She was only slightly taller than he was.

"Yes," he responded, giving her his undivided attention.

Miss Palmer waited for the other children to clear out of the room before she asked him, "Do your parents read anything at home, you know, newspapers, magazines, books or anything around the house?"

Antwan had to think about that for a minute. He knew that *Jet* and *Ebony* magazines came to the house, but he rarely saw his parents reading them. The magazines usually just sat on the coffee tables in the living room for visitors to read. His parents only seemed to read the cover captions while flipping through the pictures. His older brother and sister did the same. He rarely saw any of them sit down and read over a stretch of their free time.

Antwan spoke up and said, "My parents are too busy to read. My mom has to come home and cook and clean after work, and then help us out with our homework. And my dad is too tired when he comes home late to read anything."

Miss Palmer nodded to him again. She asked him, "Do they watch television?"

Antwan nodded back and answered, "Yeah. Everybody watches television." It only made sense to him. Why else would his family have four television sets in the house if nobody would watch them?

"So, they do have time to watch television?" Miss Palmer asked him.

Antwan caught on to her point and started to smile. The time that his family spent watching television, they could have spent reading books. Antwan came up with another idea.

He asked his teacher, "Don't you watch TV?" He was sure that everyone watched television. Watching television was an American tradition.

But Miss Palmer answered, "Rarely, and when I do, it's usually a special *news* program. But as more television networks focus their attention on entertainment and celebrity stories, even the news programs are diminished now. And I don't watch any of that mess."

Antwan heard his teacher out and said, "Well, that's *you*. Other people like to be entertained. I thought that was what television was for."

Miss Palmer nodded her head. "Okay. Well, I will tell you this; watching television for entertainment will *not* pass you into the fifth grade. Now you can let *both* of your parents know that I said that, and I still expect to see you *back* in front of my classroom to read from your book tomorrow. You had a *whole weekend* to prepare for it. So you have *no* excuses."

Miss Palmer packed up her things from her desk and then walked out of the classroom.

Antwan looked down at his *Kid Caramel* book and felt frustrated and nervous, a full day in advance.

———

That evening, Antwan sat at home with his homework spread out in front of him on the kitchen table. He was not his usual chipper self. His energy had all been consumed by thinking too much about his dilemma of having to read aloud in front of his classmates at school.

Eva, his older sister, reached out and tried to tickle him under his arms to cheer him up, only for Antwan to grumble at her and move away.

"Stop," he told her.

Eva looked at her baby brother and finally asked him, "What's wrong with you today?"

"Nothing," he grumbled again. Eva was a girl. She wouldn't understand his fear of reading. Girls liked to read.

"Well, nobody can help you if you won't even let them know what your problem is," she told to him. Then she went back to completing her own homework.

Antwan's older brother, Benjamin, never even looked up. He had his own homework to finish before Monday Night Football came on that night on ESPN. He didn't want to miss the highlights of the games played that Sunday.

Antwan kept to himself even after his homework was finished, and dinner had been served. He followed his older brother and dad into the basement to watch football on ESPN, which they always watched together.

"Man, that was a great catch, Dad," Benjamin commented to their father. They all sat on the long, comfortable couch in front of their 54-inch, color television.

"Yeah," their father grunted. He was a big man, weighing well over two hundred and fifty pounds, and who had played football in his high school days at Spingarn High School. Now he worked for a construction company and was still wearing his light blue denim outfit from work.

Antwan didn't say a word. He was still thinking about his reading assignment.

His father looked at him and asked, "How come you so quiet tonight? Anything happen at school today?"

It was a perfect question that Antwan was not yet ready to answer.

"Umm . . . well . . ."

How would he talk to his father about something he had never seen him do?

The next thing Antwan knew, his father was all up in his face about his school day.

"Umm, well, what?" his father asked him. "What happened today at school? Is there something you need to tell me? Did you get into some trouble?"

"I um . . . had to read from a book in front of my class . . . and . . . I'm not good at reading," Antwan finally admitted.

That got Benjamin's attention. He looked over at his younger brother and started to laugh.

"Shut up, Benji!" Antwan snapped at him. His feelings were hurt. That's why he didn't want to bring it up in the first place. It was embarrassing.

"You can't read, huh?" his brother continued to tease him.

"Cut it out," his father told him sternly. Then he looked back at Antwan. "So, what book are you having problems with? Because I know you can read."

Antwan said, "Yeah, but our teacher wants us to read in front of everyone. And I can't read that fast."

Benjamin was ready to laugh again before his father gave him another look that stopped him in his tracks. Then he looked at his youngest child again. "Go get me one of your books."

Antwan was confused. "Huh?"

"Go get me one of your books to read. I wanna show you a few tricks I learned when I was your age," his father told him.

Antwan cheered up and said, "Okay."

He dashed back up to the kitchen to find his back pack and pulled his *Kid Caramel* book out. His sister Eva watched him in confusion.

"Why are you all happy about getting a book?" She had never seen that from her brother before.

He ignored her and ran back down into the basement with it. When he reached his father on the couch and handed the book to him, his father made room for Antwan to sit down next to him.

He looked the book over and nodded. "*Kid Caramel*. We didn't have any Black books when I was a kid in school. But I used to like *Curious George*."

Benjamin overheard him and began to smile. He had rarely seen his father with a book in his hand either. Their mother had done most of the reading and helped with homework in their household, while their father worked hard to pay the bills, fix things, protect the house, and then relax in the basement.

He told Antwan, "Now watch my finger move as I read. 'It was the first day of school. Actually it was more of a parade of new clothes, notebooks, rules, and sneakers . . .'"

Antwan's father continued to read while he followed his large brown finger under each word that he read.

"The key is to keep it moving," he said. "Don't get stopped at one word. Let your mind and tongue say what you *think* the word is and then move on to the next word."

Antwan asked him, "But what if you get the word wrong?"

His father told him, "As long as you know what the next word is, you can figure it out sometimes as you go along. But if you stop cold at each word, then you're stuck. So you always want to think about reading the whole sentence and not just one word by itself. And when you get a word wrong, the teacher will correct you once you're finished. But at least you got through it, right?"

Antwan nodded, thinking about how he stopped after every single word, and how it took him forever to read that way. So he figured his father's finger technique made sense.

"Here, you try it," his father told him, handing over the book. "Start at the third paragraph."

Antwan held the book open in his hands while his brother and father watched him.

"Benjamin, put that TV on mute," his father told his brother. Antwan was even shocked by that. His father loved the football highlights too.

Antwan placed his finger under the first word and began to read, "Shark-tooth shoved the . . . kid next to him in-to . . . a walk. Creepy . . . Timmy was wiping some-thing from his nose . . . on his shirt."

Antwan was not reading as smoothly as his father had, but at least he wasn't getting stuck at every word as long as usual.

"You see how that feels?" his father asked him. "Now you practice that to yourself out loud."

Antwan continued to read aloud with his finger while his father continued to watch the football highlights at a much lower volume than usual. Every few big words, his father would correct him without even seeing it. Antwan was impressed with that. He had no idea his father could read so well. So he decided to ask him about it.

"Hey Dad, did kids used to tease you in school when you were my age?"

"About reading?" his father assumed. "Oh yeah, all the time. But I had to learn how to do it. We all have to learn how to read. It's just like riding a bike."

"But I never see you reading anything around the house," Antwan said.

"Yeah, and you never see me riding a bike either," his father responded with a chuckle. But that doesn't mean I don't know how to ride one."

Antwan paused before he asked his father a harder question. "Are girls better readers than guys?"

His father stopped and stared at him for a minute before he broke out laughing. "You know, girls seem to be more involved in reading than guys are, but I wouldn't exactly call them *better readers*. They just read *more*. But guys tend to read more complicated things. For instance, whenever there are any instructions to put something together, your mother brings it right to me. But if you're talking about reading books, newspapers and stories and things, your mother and sister tend to read that stuff a little bit more. But not the business and sports pages. They give that to me.

"So, men and women tend to read differently, that's all," he stated. "Nevertheless, we *all* need to know *how* to read. And I don't care what nobody says about that. So you practice what I taught you, and you give a better effort in class the next time. You hear me?"

Antwan nodded to him and smiled. He didn't expect his father to support reading at all, since he rarely saw him do it. But since he *did* support reading, Antwan decided to make a stronger effort to read better himself.

"In fact," his father told him, "I guess we *all* need to start reading a little more around here." Then he snapped his fingers at his older son. "Benjamin, go on upstairs and get the sports page so we can read what they said about the Redskins' loss yesterday."

Benjamin smiled and ran upstairs to grab the *Washington Post* sports section. And Antwan continued to read from his book, confident that he would do a better job reading aloud in his class the next day. It would be just like climbing back on his bike.

Chapter 4

Jamaica Boys

Oneal, Ernest, Daniel, and Bulldog all waited before they finally decided to walk up to the front door of their neighbor's house.

"Come on, let's just go get him," Ernest told his friends, tired of waiting. "He should be ready to come out by now."

Each kid was carrying a small sack of marbles. It was another bright and sunny morning of pleasant summertime weather on the Caribbean island of Jamaica.

The four friends were all ready to meet up with their fifth friend, Stevie, for their usual, fun-filled and adventurous day in their neighborhood. Ranging in ages from 10 to 12, the boys all lived on the same street and attended the same grade school. Before they could make it to Stevie's house, Stevie overheard them and cracked the door open to sneak outside, just as Oneal's long, brown arm reached up to ring the bell.

"Hey, let's go," Stevie told him in haste.

Oneal jumped back, surprised and said, "I was just about to ring your bell."

Stevie shook his head and frowned at him. "No, you might wake up my mom. Let's go." He then thought of a way to rush them all from his house.

"I bet you can't beat me up the street," he said before he took off running.

Ernest, Daniel, Bulldog, and Oneal raced after him. At 10 years old, Stevie was the smallest kid in their crew. So it didn't take long for the others to zip right by him. Ernest ran past him first, followed by Daniel, Bulldog, and finally Oneal. They all stopped once they reached the dirt circle where they liked to play marbles.

"Boy, you're way slow, *bredjin*," Ernest teased Stevie. Ernest was the second youngest kid at 11, and he was always ready to brag about his quick feet.

"Yeah, but we all beat you, my *yute*. You came second to last," Daniel told him. At 12, he was one of the older boys, a sturdy youth with brown, bulging calves and shoulder muscles that stretched his royal blue tank-top.

"You all had a head start on me. But I tied Oneal for first," Bulldog added to their argument. He was stockier than Daniel, so much that he bent slightly forward when he walked, earning him the Bulldog nickname. And he wasn't turning 12 for another three months.

bredjin - Jamaican dialect for brother or kin
yute - Jamaican dialect for my youth, or young friend

"I wasn't even running my fastest," Stevie told them. "I only did that to get away from my house before my mom called me in to clean my room."

"No, no, no, you're a liar, my *yute*. You were running as fast as you could," Ernest argued. He didn't want Stevie to try and snatch away his small victory.

Stevie frowned again. He said, "Ernest, I'll beat you any day of the week, around the whole scheme."

"Let's do it right now then, *bredjin*," Ernest challenged him.

"I'm in too," Bulldog stated.

"Me too," Daniel added.

Oneal listened to all of their bickering and smiled with no comment. He was the oldest and tallest of the bunch, with long arms and legs. He felt he could easily beat them all in a race. So there was no need for him to argue.

"So, you had us all racing for nothing, just to get you away from cleaning your room," Oneal summed up for himself.

Stevie grinned at him mischievously. "Everybody got their marbles?" he asked his friends.

The boys all held up their palm-sized dark bags of marbles, which were secured with a white drawstring to keep them inside.

"You ready to lose them?" Oneal asked.

Stevie said, "We'll see," and he kneeled down next to the dirt circle.

The other boys kneeled down beside him and began to select their marbles from their bags. Stevie waited and watched them before he pulled out a blue marble with a yellow cat's eye through the middle. His friends all stopped and stared at it.

"When did you get that one?" Daniel asked him. He wanted Stevie's attractive marble for his own collection.

Stevie smiled and answered, "I got it yesterday. My aunt gave me the money for helping her to clean out the yard."

"Well, you better get ready to cry when I break it then," Oneal warned him.

Ernest looked alarmed. He asked, "Are we just knocking them out the circle or playing to break 'em? I don't want to play to break 'em. I just got these new marbles."

Bulldog took out his selected marbles for the circle and said, "Well, don't play then, scared boy."

"I'm not scared," Ernest argued.

"Then put your marbles in the circle then, *bredjin*," Stevie told him.

Ernest took a deep breath and began to dig through his bag for the least attractive of his marbles.

Daniel said, "They're only marbles. Come on, my *yute*. You can get more at the store."

Ernest's careful selection was slowing up their game. Everyone else had selected their first marbles for the circle already. They each selected three.

"I'm first to shoot," Stevie said, holding his gold and blue cat's eye marble in his hands.

"Why you get to go first?" Ernest asked him.

"Because I just do. Now let's play," Stevie snapped at him. Before Ernest could let out another word, Stevie plucked his marble into the circle and cracked one of Ernest's marbles wide open.

CLACK!

He knocked two of the other 14 marbles out of the circle with his strong pluck.

The boys all got excited. "Whoa, that marble is hard!"

Ernest looked on with horror and protested. "See, boy, why you do that? Why you go after mine first?" He had tears in his eyes.

"Aw, stop crying, *bredjin*," Bulldog told him. "Wait until you see what I'm gonna do when it's my turn to shoot."

They each took turns plucking marbles out of the circle while trying to break them. By the time they were almost done, seven marbles had been broken, but Stevie's cat's eye was still holding strong.

"Down to the last two, Stevie, boy," Oneal told him.

"Yeah, and I'm gonna win again," Daniel called out. He had knocked out the most marbles, but it was Stevie's turn to pluck again.

Stevie aimed and plucked his strong marble again. It broke yet another marble and ricocheted back into the circle.

"Aw, *bredjin*, that marble is *tough*!" Bulldog said excitedly. "Boy, you gotta good one."

Stevie spent no time celebrating. He immediately stood up from their game of marbles and said, "Let's go get our kites."

The boys liked the idea, so they collected the rest of their marbles into their bags and agreed with him.

"Let's race to 'em," Daniel challenged. They all took off running to a backyard hiding place at Daniel's house to gather their kites.

Stevie was pressed to show Ernest how fast he could really run. Only Oneal ran past him this time.

"Now who's the fastest?" Stevie asked everyone.

"I am, my *yute*," Oneal announced with a grin.

Stevie looked up at him and nodded. "Well, who's the second fastest?"

Bulldog didn't want to hear any of that. "Aw, man, I tripped," he commented.

"Yeah, and then he bumped into me," Ernest added.

"I was still collecting my marbles," said Daniel. "I didn't even get a chance to run."

"Excuses, excuses," Stevie told them all. "But I beat all of you."

They began to gather their kites made of pasted newspaper on bamboo sticks with long strings attached. Each kid had his own recognizable section of the paper with his individual kite design.

"My kite still looks the best," said Daniel, proud of his crafty work.

"So what? You spent all day working on it. Mine would look that good too if I spent all day on it," Oneal responded. Daniel was the main kite maker. He had shown everyone else how to improve their kites.

"Let's play kite wars again," Stevie suggested. Each boy would attach thorny stems or pointy sticks to their kites to damage an opponent's kite in the air.

"Your kite never wins," Bulldog told Stevie.

"So, it's just for the fun of it, right Stevie?" Ernest asked him.

Stevie's kite was already damaged and in need of repair. He picked it up. He said, "Yeah, it's only paper and sticks."

"That's easy for you to say," Daniel responded. "But I like my kites."

"Just like I like my marbles," Ernest spoke up. "So, come on, scared boy. You told me not to cry about breaking my marbles. So don't cry about your kite."

Daniel snapped, "That was Bulldog. I didn't say that."

"Well, come on, let's fly them," Bulldog urged. "You can always make another kite. Daniel, boy, you're a kite expert."

Oneal laughed and said, "Yeah, he is."

They then ran off toward the open field of dirt across the street, where a half dozen stray goats roamed.

"Aw, boy, those stupid goats are in the way again," Ernest commented.

Stevie's eyes lit up with another idea. "Let's chase them away and see who can catch up to them the fastest."

Not wanting to be beaten again, Bulldog took off running with his kite string in hand. And in his eagerness not to be beaten by Stevie in another race, Bulldog unwittingly banged his kite across the ground.

"You just broke your kite already," Daniel told him. Bulldog didn't even care enough to slow down. He ran down the first stray goat and tagged him on the back. Then he sprinted for the second and third goats as the animals all scattered in different directions.

"Don't go after that mean one," Oneal tried to warn Bulldog as he approached the largest and slowest goat.

Bulldog was so fearless and determined that he smacked the goat across his back right before it turned and tried to bite his hand.

"Whoa, he just missed you," Stevie said, amazed by the goat's quick reflexes. But Bulldog was already chasing the next goat. He ran the goats all down before his friends had the chance to try to match him.

"Now, who's the best goat chaser?" Bulldog boasted, proud of himself.

"You better wash your hands before you touch me," Oneal warned him again. "You might catch a goat disease."

The other boys began to laugh as Bulldog looked at his hands with concern. He shook his head and said, "You can't catch a disease just from touching."

"Yes, you can, too," Ernest told him. "You know that crazy old man who sleeps on the streets at night. Well, he touches goats all the time. That's why he's crazy now."

Bulldog argued, "No he's not. He's just crazy because he's crazy. It don't have nothing to do with goats."

"Well, you need to fix your kite now to play war with," Daniel reminded him. "Look at it."

Bulldog's kite was ripped in half from his desperate running in the open field. It was unable to fly anymore. So Bulldog said, "Fix it then, expert."

"Okay, wait one minute," Daniel told him. He took off running toward his house again to grab more newspaper and paste to repair his friend's kite. In the meantime, Stevie looked down and picked up a couple of empty soda bottles from the ground.

"I'm gonna collect bottles until he gets back," he stated.

Oneal said, "Yeah, we can sell them and buy some more marbles." He dropped his kite to the ground and looked across the open field to a loaded trash barrel before he took off running for it.

"Wait, that was my idea," Stevie protested.

Oneal kept running and hollered back, "Thanks, my *yute*!" They all knew they could never catch Oneal with a head start. So Ernest turned and looked for another trash barrel to raid. Once he found another one, he was up against Bulldog and Stevie to make his move for it.

Watching Ernest and Bulldog take off for the second trash barrel before he could, Stevie came up with another idea. He stood his two soda bottles on the ground and gathered several rocks to throw at them.

"What are you doing?" Oneal asked him.

Stevie told him, "I'm testing my aim," and continued throwing his rocks at the bottles until he finally broke one.

Oneal shook his head while holding an armful of empty soda and Jamaican beer bottles. He asked Stevie, "Why break the bottles when we can sell them?"

Stevie ignored him and kept throwing rocks at the second bottle. Once Bulldog and Ernest arrived with their armful of bottles, they watched Stevie and decided to test their own aim with rocks. But Stevie stopped them.

"Don't throw at my bottle," he warned. "Use your own bottles."

Bulldog and Ernest both froze and looked at each other.

Bulldog said, "I'm only breaking one." He walked over to set up only one of his collected bottles.

Oneal was still uninterested. He said, "I'm not breaking any of mine."

But Ernest was all in for it. He walked over and set up one of his bottles to aim at with a rock. He broke it on the first throw.

"I bet you can't do that again," Stevie said.

Ernest looked at him and said, "Watch me."

He walked over and set up another bottle and broke it again with a lone rock.

"Whoa. I didn't know you could throw like that," Bulldog told him. He continued to miss his own bottle.

Oneal, watching that, walked over and grabbed a rock to throw at Bulldog's bottle and just barely missed it.

Bulldog said, "Hey, *bredjin*, like Stevie said, you use your own bottles. You got more than all of us."

Oneal thought about it and decided, "All right, watch me."

By the time he set up one of his bottles to break, Daniel made it back over to them to repair Bulldog's kite.

"What are you all doing?" he asked his friends.

"What does it look like we're doing? We're testing our aim," Stevie told him.

Daniel looked and said, "I can do that." He walked toward Ernest's collection of bottles to grab one.

Ernest pushed him away and said, "Hey, you get your own bottles to break."

Daniel stopped and looked around for some other bottles to collect. He finally spotted one that was too far away for him to want to walk to it.

"For what?" he said. He looked at all the extra bottles Oneal had in his collection. "Oneal can give me one of his bottles. Look at all of them."

Oneal frowned at him and said, "I'm gonna sell my bottles. I'm only breaking this one."

Daniel said, "Well, let me break one."

"No," Oneal told him.

Stevie still hadn't broken his second bottle yet, so he looked at Daniel and gave him a nice sized rock to throw.

"Go ahead. See if you can break my bottle then," he told him.

Daniel smiled and took the rock from his friend's hand. "Thanks."

On his first throw, Daniel smashed the bottle that Stevie had continued to miss after seven throws. That gave Stevie another idea.

"Hey, let's see who can break the most bottles between Daniel, Ernest, and Oneal," Stevie suggested. "I bet you three bottles that Daniel can break one before Ernest does."

Oneal looked at him and said, "Bet me with what? You don't even have any more bottles."

Stevie thought fast and responded, "I'll bet you with Bulldog's bottles."

Bulldog looked at him and said, "No, you're not betting him with *my* bottles. You get your *own* bottles to bet."

"But if you and Ernest win, then you can get three of Oneal's bottles," Stevie said.

Bulldog stopped and thought about it. "Oh, so it's me and Ernest against Oneal and Daniel then?"

Oneal caught on to that and said, "No way. I want Ernest on my team. Daniel just got lucky. Ernest has a better aim."

"Well, Ernest can bet for Daniel's kite then," Stevie said.

Bulldog thought about that and said, "I want to bet for Daniel's kite. I'm the one with the broken one."

"I thought we were betting for bottles. I'm not betting for my kite," Daniel said.

Stevie said, "Why, are you scared, *bredjin*? Once you win some bottles, then you can bet bottles."

"All right, boy, I'm not scared. Let's do it. I can always make another kite anyway," Daniel nodded and said.

Bulldog smiled from ear to ear, believing that he had a good deal to win Daniel's prized kite.

But then Ernest protested. "Wait a minute. I should be the one to bet against Daniel. I'm the one throwing the rocks."

Bulldog looked at the six bottles that Ernest had left to his twelve, and he decided to up the bet.

He said, "Okay, I'll bet five bottles for Daniel's kite then."

Ernest was confused. He said, "Well, you throw your own rocks against him then. Why you use me?"

"Because your aim is better than mine," Bulldog told him.

"Well, let me bet him then," Ernest insisted.

"Come on, boy, let's do it already," Oneal told them. They were all wasting time arguing.

Stevie said, "Okay, I'll bet with Daniel then. And you all can put up five bottles. And if Daniel loses, he gives up his kite to Bulldog, and then he makes better kites for you and Oneal."

Everyone liked the idea but Daniel. "Wait a minute, boy. What do I get?" he said.

Stevie said, "You get to split fifteen bottles with me."

"Why, what did you do?" Bulldog said. He didn't see the logic in Daniel splitting anything with Stevie.

Stevie said, "I came up with the idea. He wouldn't win any bottles if it wasn't for me."

"Come on, let's do it then." said Oneal. "Ernest is gonna win anyway." So he set up his five bottles in a pile.

Daniel asked, "And what if I lose? Then I'm going to be doing all the work by myself."

"I'll help you build the kites then. Is that fair?" Stevie said.

Daniel begin to think about it, and before he could make up his mind, Stevie said, "All right Ernest, you go first."

"Why does he go first?" Daniel whined.

No sooner than he had asked the question, Ernest tossed his first rock at a bottle and missed.

Stevie turned to Daniel and said, "See, now it's your turn. All you have to do is break it and we win."

Daniel smiled and agreed to it. The pressure was on the other friends now.

"He's not gonna break it," Oneal repeated.

Daniel heard that and tossed his rock with determination. The rock zipped straight at the center of the bottle and broke it right through the middle.

Stevie jumped up and down. "Yeah, *bredjin*! I told you

we'd win, boy!" he shouted. He began to collect his bottles immediately.

Ernest said, "Wait a minute. That's not fair. Let's bet again."

Stevie stopped suddenly and listened to the sound of the air. He said, "My mom is calling me."

Everyone stopped and listened with him but heard nothing.

Bulldog spoke up about it first. "No she's not."

The next second, a loud cry rang out from Stevie's front door, "STEEE-VEEEE! GET IN HERE, BOY! You have work to do this morning!"

"I told you," Stevie said with a grin. He gathered his share of the bottles and took off running toward his house.

When he reached his doorway, his mother asked him, "What are you doing out here so early in the morning? You know you have work to do before you go out and play."

Stevie showed his mother the bottles and said, "I know, but we wanted to collect bottles early before the other boys could beat us to it. Then we sell the bottles back to the store for food for when we get hungry."

His mother looked down at the seven bottles in his arms. "Boy, those bottles are filthy. You have to wash them up before you sell them to anyone."

Stevie said, "Okay," and walked into the house behind her.

Ten minutes later, Oneal, Ernest, Daniel, and Bulldog were bored and waiting outside of Stevie's house for him to finish his daily chores and come back out to play.

Finally, Bulldog smiled through their silence. He said, "Stevie sure is slick. But man . . . it sure is boring without him."

They all laughed before Oneal said, "Yeah, and when he comes back out, we're gonna finish our kite wars, and then have milk box car races again like yesterday. I have the best milk box car of all of us."

Daniel frowned and said, "We'll see about that. Just wait 'til Stevie comes back out."

Bulldog nodded and said, "Okay. Let's all get our milk box cars and wait for Stevie to come back. Because I want to win my bottles back."

All of a sudden, Oneal looked around at his friends and asked them all, "How come we're always waiting for Stevie anyway?"

Ernest agreed, "Yeah, why are we always waiting for him?" We can have our kite wars."

"Because he has my bottles," Bulldog said.

But Daniel said, "Because . . . he has the best ideas." And he had just won Daniel eight free bottles.

Oneal didn't like the sound of that either. After all, he was the oldest, and Stevie had just gotten away with winning five of his hard-earned bottles. "We can have our own ideas. He's not the only one with ideas. Let's keep having fun without him," Oneal said.

Bulldog nodded and agreed with Oneal and Ernest. He said, "Yeah, we should start our own kite wars and milk box car races. And if Stevie misses it, then that's him. But why should we stand around and do nothing waiting for him all the time?"

Finally, Daniel agreed, too. After all, he loved flying kites. "Okay. So, who's gonna be the last one to get their kite?"

"Ernest is. He the slowest," said Oneal.

"We'll see," Ernest challenged.

In a flash, they all took off running again. Bulldog told Daniel, "And you still have to help me fix mine," as they prepared to enjoy the rest of their day with their own plans and ideas.

Chapter 5

IT TAKES TIME

"**C**ome on, man, hurry up. You always taking all day," Demetrius said to his friend Brandon at the West Charlotte YMCA summer camp. They were still at the art station, but it was time for their outside recess break, and Demetrius was pressed to get all his play time minutes.

However, Brandon ignored him and continued to connect the detailed lines of his drawing of an original cartoon character. He didn't even like to speak while he was drawing. "One more minute," he responded.

Demetrius watched him impatiently for another couple of minutes before he decided that enough was enough. Brandon just refused to move with any urgency.

"All right, man, forget it, then. I'm going outside," Demetrius finally told him.

Brandon didn't bother to tell him good-bye. He was too focused on his artwork. Even one of the camp counselors noticed his slow pace.

"Ah, Brandon, you know you can finish your drawing after you come back in, don't you?" Mrs. Addison asked him. She was one of the head counselors at the summer camp.

Brandon barely looked up at her. He said, "I know, but I don't want to go out."

Mrs. Addison gave him another look and shrugged her shoulders. "Okay."

Brandon continued, very carefully, to connect the small lines of Zarf, his alien space man character, in an action scene. His idea was to create a galaxy-flying hero with blue skin, long ears and a short body, who saved worlds from destruction and all forces of evil. Brandon planned to draw his hero in a white space suit with gold and black trim. Instead of a nose or a mouth, small oxygen and moisture holes in his hands would help him to breathe and consume water. And Zarf would speak to all living organisms through mental telepathy.

When Brandon's age group of 26 11- and 12-year-old campers returned from their free play outside, he was still at work and nearly finished with his drawing.

Demetrius asked him, "Boy, you're still sitting in here? What's wrong with you, B? You can finish that thing any time."

Brandon smiled and said, "I'm almost finished now."

The key word was "almost." Brandon never finished anything in haste. Judging for himself, Demetrius looked down at his friend's alien hero and realized that Brandon *was* almost finished. All he had left to do was color him in.

"Hey, that looks cool," another camper commented, looking over Demetrius' shoulder at Brandon's artwork.

His curiosity made the other campers want to peek.

"Let me see it," they all exclaimed, crowding around Brandon at his art station.

Mrs. Addison examined his nearly finished artwork for herself. She nodded and said, "That *does* look good, Brandon. You are really gifted with your drawings."

"Yeah, he *takes* long enough," Demetrius teased.

"I just want to do it right," Brandon responded with a smile.

"There's nothing wrong with that," Mrs. Addison told him.

One of the other campers asked him, "But what is that supposed to be?"

"His name is Zarf," Brandon answered, "and he's an intergalactic protector of endangered worlds."

After hearing that, some of the campers began to chuckle.

"Yeah, he has a big imagination. There's no such thing as a world protector in real life," one of the boys cracked.

"That's okay," Mrs. Addison said. "The imagination is all about coming up with things that are new, or that haven't been done before. That's why we have you guys writing so much and completing so many creative projects this summer instead of just playing all day. We want to get your minds ready to start thinking about the infinite possibilities of the creative world that we live in."

She smiled and added, "There just may be some alien lifeform out there somewhere. Has any of us ever been in outer space?"

"No," the campers answered her question with chuckles.

"All right then. So none of us really knows," she told them.

After their art instruction had ended, a visiting music teacher introduced the campers to the joy of playing different musical instruments.

The music teacher—an older, brown-haired woman—worked at a music store where kids were taught how to play drums, guitar, violin, piano, trumpet and the clarinet. She brought various instrument with her to showcase to the campers.

She started by introducing herself. "Hello everyone, my name is Beverly Packard, and I work as a lesson coordinator at The Art & Music Center here in Charlotte, where we teach kids the fundamentals of playing a number of different musical instruments. Now how many of you have had lessons or play a musical instrument?" she asked.

Almost half of the campers' hands went up, including Brandon's.

"And what instruments do you all play?" she asked the raised hands.

They went down the line, calling out the instruments they played:

"I play the piano."

"The drums."

"The drums."

"The violin."

"The flute."

"My mom teaches me to play the piano."

"I play the trumpet."

"The drums."

When it was Brandon's turn, he was the only camper in the room to answer, "The acoustic guitar."

"Oh, so we have one guitar player, one violinist, several drummers, several pianists, a few trumpet players, and a flutist," Beverly recounted. "Well, they are all lovely instruments. And since some of you have had lessons, I don't want to put any of you on the spot, necessarily, but . . . if any of you would be willing to play, I would love to hear some of what you have learned."

After hearing her challenge, the kids stepped up to volunteer in a hurry. They were all eager to show off their instrumental skills to their fellow campers. So, one by one, they walked up front to play the instruments that Beverly had brought for them. When it was Brandon's turn, he sat up front with the acoustic guitar on his lap and played it better than anyone in the room had imagined. They were all impressed. Brandon sure didn't seem like a musician to them. But after he played the guitar, they all had an heightened level of respect for him.

"Wow!" Beverly responded. "That was really good. How long have you had guitar lessons?"

"Since I was five," Brandon answered.

That surprised Beverly as well. "Since you were *five*?" she repeated. "Well, that's nearly half of your life, isn't it?"

Brandon smiled and nodded.

"Well, that takes a lot of patience to be able to learn to play the guitar at five. It's a lot of repetition, right?" Beverly asked him.

He said, "Yeah, for years I had to learn how to use, my fingers on the strings over and over again."

Beverly nodded and said, "Yeah, I know. And that's a lot to ask of a five year old."

Brandon added, "I was the first five year old that my instructor ever taught."

"Well, I bet he's proud of you now, isn't he?" the music instructor assumed.

"My teacher's a woman," Brandon corrected her.

Beverly, a woman instructor herself, was now embarrassed by her assumption. "Oh, well, excuse me. I'm sorry," she said with a chuckle. "Women can teach boys, too. What's wrong with me? Well, I bet *she's* proud of you then," she said. "*Very* proud."

Demetrius sat there and took it all in. His mother had asked him if he wanted to play musical instruments several times. And he had always tuned her down.

"You have to practice too much," he had complained to his mother. "Brandon practices on that guitar all the time."

Demetrius' mother told him, "That's because he *wants* to, not because he *has* to. You don't have to practice all the time if you don't want to. But you *do* have to take lessons to learn."

Demetrius heard his mother use the words "lessons to learn," and all he could think about was the amount of time that Brandon had spent away from doing other fun things, like skate boarding, playing video games, or hanging out at the playground. So he declined.

"No, that's all right. I don't want to learn."

But after seeing how good his friend had become at playing the guitar, Demetrius was inspired to rethink taking music lessons. And as soon as his mother arrived to pick him up from camp that day, he was all over her with his new idea.

"Hey Mom, I think I'm ready to take music lessons now," Demetrius announced from the passenger's seat in his mother's car.

His mother was surprised. She looked at him and asked, "Why? Why all of a sudden?" She had her own ideas about it, like most moms do, but she waited for her son to explain it in his own words.

He said, "They had a music teacher bring instruments and talk about taking private lessons at camp today. Then she let people play the instruments, and Brandon played the guitar."

His mother began to smile. "And now you want to learn," she commented.

Demetrius smiled back at her. "Yeah. I mean, it's better late than never, right?"

As they headed into traffic on their way home, his mother nodded to him. "So, what instrument do you want to learn to play?"

"The acoustic guitar," Demetrius responded excitedly. Then he quickly backed up and changed his mind. "No, the *electric* guitar. That's the one's that the rock band people play."

His mother continued to stare at him. She asked, "So, you wanna be in a rock band now?"

Demetrius grinned, imagining being front stage with thousands of wild and crazy fans screaming at him.

"Yeah," he answered. "I could be in the band with Brandon. They have two and three guitar players sometimes."

His mother nodded again, feeling comfortable with the idea. "Well, the electric guitar is a little more expensive than the acoustic. The acoustic guitar only needs a pick to play it, but the electric needs cords and an amplifier." She said, "Maybe you should just learn how to *play* a guitar first."

"And I can do that on the electric guitar," Demetrius insisted.

"Yeah, a guitar that you can't even play without electricity," his mother argued. She said, "But we'll see."

"When?" Demetrius asked her. "Today?"

His mother looked back at him and frowned. "No, I have grocery shopping to do this evening."

"Tomorrow, then?" he pressed her.

His mother didn't like the hasty pressure he was giving her, but she nodded to him anyway. "Okay, tomorrow after camp, we'll visit the music store."

"Yes!" Demetrius exclaimed, with all smiles.

The next day at camp, Demetrius told Brandon all about his idea. "My mom's taking me to get signed up for guitar lessons today," he said.

Brandon warned him, "You'll need to learn how to play all of the chords first. It took me *years* to do that."

"Well, maybe I'll learn it faster than you."

Brandon heard his friend say that, and he started smiling. "Does that mean you're going to practice then?"

Demetrius hated even hearing the word "practice." He answered, "My mom said I don't have to practice as much as you do," he commented. "I can practice when I want to."

Brandon listened to that and continued to grin. He said, "Okay, if you say so," he replied with a shrug. That was all Brandon planned to say about it. And if Demetrius was serious about learning how to play the guitar, he would find out real fast how hard it would be without practice and dedication.

———

When Demetrius and his mother showed up at the music store to buy a guitar and to sign him up for lessons, they hit a road block.

One of the sales clerks took them to the guitar section and pointed out an electric guitar starter kit that cost close to $400.

"Of course, this isn't the best sound that you're gonna get, but it's at least something to start him off with," he said.

Demetrius' mother looked at the acoustic guitars that were hanging down from hooks right next to them, and she noticed that the price tags started as low as $79. The electric guitars had starting prices closer to $300, without an electric chord, a carrying case, or an amplifier.

So his mother asked, "What about these acoustic guitars. What quality are they?"

The sales clerk changed his tone and became more enthusiastic. He said, "Oh, now you can buy a quality acoustic guitar right at $100. But the better electric guitars are gonna cost you."

"And the lessons are close to $100 a month too, right?" she asked him.

The salesclerk nodded in agreement. "Yeah, that's about right."

"And he still has to learn how to play the basic notes on any guitar, right?" His mother was asking all the right questions.

The salesclerk nodded again. "That's right."

Demetrius saw where his mother was going with her conversation, and he started to complain before she said another word.

"But Mom, I don't want to learn on the acoustic guitar, I want to learn with electric."

His mother asked the salesclerk politely, "Could you give us a minute, please?"

"Oh, sure," he said and backed away from them.

Demetrius' mother looked down at him and said, "Now look, Demetrius, I am not spending over $500 in here today for you to learn how to play the electric guitar, when you still have to learn the notes first. So, if you really want to learn how to play a guitar, then you need to start off with a cheaper acoustic one and prove to yourself that you really want to do this. Because if I pay $500 in here, and then I hear you complaining about not wanting to practice or come to the lessons . . ."

Demetrius cut his mother off and said, "I'm not *gonna* complain."

"Good. Then don't complain now," his mother said, sternly. "Because the reality is, the man already told us that you can learn to play on a quality *acoustic* guitar for *half* the price that it would cost for you to learn on a *bad* sounding electric."

"But yesterday you said I could play the electric," Demetrius pouted.

"No, I did not," his mother snapped at him. "I only *asked* you what you wanted to play, and I said 'we'll *see*'. But I am not buying *any* electric guitar for you until I can see, for a least a *year*, that you're really into this. So you pick out one of these acoustics and take the lessons, or I'm not doing it."

His mother had put her foot down and was not bending, so Demetrius took a deep breath and thought it over. The acoustic guitar with a year of lessons or nothing?

He finally sighed and said, "Okay."

"Are you sure?" his mother asked him. "Because I'm not forcing you into this, Demetrius. If you don't want to do it, then don't waste my time or my money."

"I *do* want to do it," he spoke it.

"All right then," she told him. "Now pick out the acoustic guitar that you like."

When Demetrius told Brandon that his mother wouldn't let him buy an electric guitar until he had taken a year of lessons on the acoustic first, Brandon forced himself to hold in a laugh. He knew it all along.

"Don't worry about it, D," he comforted. "I'm going to be moving up to the electric guitar in another year too."

Demetrius heard that and got excited. He asked, "So you want to play the electric guitar too?"

"Yeah," Brandon told him. "I can't *wait* to play the electric guitar. I've been waiting for *years* to play. But I still had to learn how to play the chords first." He said, "And I also want to paint and make my own comics, but I have to learn how to draw first. So all the times that you tease me about practicing, I don't mind it, because I know that everything good takes time, unless you want to be what my dad calls an 'unfortunate lucky person.'"

Demetrius frowned and repeated, "Unfortunate lucky person? What is that?"

Brandon smiled and explained. "My dad told me that sometimes people get lucky opportunities without really being good. But then they end up suffering because everyone else moves right past them, and they never find out how to catch up. He talks about musicians being one-hit wonders and stuff, or going through burn out, or being stuck in one place because they were never really good at what they were doing."

"So, when some people get lucky by finding success too fast, they end up being unfortunate because they're not prepared for it, and then they fall back down. But my dad told me to be a good artist, or to be good in anything, it just takes time to learn. And when you take your time to learn, you never panic when things don't go right, you just slow down, think about it, and fix it."

Demetrius listened to his friend and understood that he had no choice. He would have to learn at a slower pace than what he wanted. He smiled and said, "I guess we can practice our guitars together now."

Brandon smiled back. "Okay. Now I'll see how much practice you can take."

Demetrius heard his challenge and said, "Bring it on, then! I can practice. You watch me."

Brandon continued to smile. He knew that doing the actual work of *practice* was a whole lot harder than just talking about it. And now Demetrius had a whole year to prove that he would be able to stick to the program.

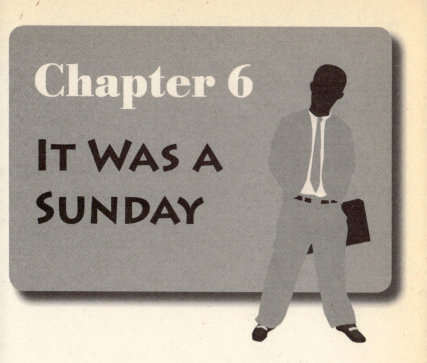

Chapter 6

It Was a Sunday

"Wayne, would you hurry up and put your suit on, boy. What in the world are you doing?" Odessa Ellerbee asked, as she stood inside the doorway of her son's bedroom.

Wayne, the oldest child of three, was still wearing his boxers and a clean white tank top. His dark, pinstriped suit, mint green, button-up shirt, and green and white striped tie were all resting on his bed for him to wear to church that morning. But instead of getting dressed, Wayne was sitting up on his bed and laughing to himself, reading the comics section of the Sunday newspaper.

"All right," he told his mother without budging. He only had four more comic strips to read before he would be ready to go.

"She means *now*, Wayne," the booming voice of his father commanded from the hallway.

Wayne closed the newspaper and jumped up to pull on his dress pants. "Okay," he whimpered.

Anthony Ellerbee, a towering brown man at six foot and four inches, stepped inside his son's doorway behind his wife and said, "If I hear another word come out of your mouth without you getting dressed, you gon' have to do some praying right here and right now to get me off of you. Now you get those clothes on, brush your teeth, comb your hair, and get downstairs with your brother and sister."

Everyone but Wayne was dressed and ready to go.

When his parents walked away from his doorway, Wayne hurried to get his clothes on. Once he was fully dressed, he pulled the comics section into the bathroom with him so he could read the rest of it while he brushed his teeth and combed his hair. He knew his father wouldn't let him take the comics inside the car with him. He would be taking his personal bible to church instead.

Wayne arrived downstairs dressed, groomed and ready to go with his bible in hand just before his mother had the chance to call out for him.

"Boy, you're getting on my last nerves with your tardiness. Now when we say we're ready to go, that's what we mean," she huffed at him. Then she looked at his younger sister and brother, who had both gotten dressed nearly an hour ago.

"Now what example are you setting for both of them?" she demanded to know. "Have you ever stopped to think about that?"

Wayne frowned and said, "But Mom, you and Dad help them get dressed, that's why they're always ready."

"No, they don't. I dress myself," Cynthia, his younger sister, argued.

"And Dad only helps me with my tie and shoes," his younger brother Dalvin added.

His mother said, "Wayne, I don't believe how immature you can be sometimes. You're gonna sit up here and start and argument with them, *knowing* that you're the oldest."

Mrs. Ellerbee was so upset with her oldest child that she pushed him toward the doorway. "Go on outside and get in the car," she told him.

Wayne stumbled forward toward the front door and mumbled under his breath, "I didn't ask to be the oldest."

"What was that?" his mother asked him as they all made it outside the door.

"Nothing," Wayne responded tartly.

His father was pulling the family minivan out of the garage so they could all climb in at the edge of the driveway.

Wayne got in first and hurried to the third row of back seats. Cynthia climbed in behind him and followed his lead. By the time Dalvin climbed in, there was not much room left in the back.

"I wanna sit back there," the baby brother pouted.

"Aw, boy, stop whining and sit in the middle," Wayne told him.

Dalvin tried in vain to squeeze into the back seat anyway, only to have Wayne push him forward.

"Stop, boy," he complained with a shove.

His brother cried out, "Mom, Wayne pushed me."

Mrs. Ellerbee turned to face her children from the front passenger seat and asked, "Wayne, why can't you act like you have any *sense*, boy? Is it that important for you to sit in the back?"

"No, but I got here first," he answered.

His father overheard his response from the wheel and shook his head. He would have to work overtime to improve his son's behavior. Wayne would be turning 13 soon.

To stop himself from thinking about his son's immaturity, Mr. Ellerbee turned on the radio to the Atlanta, Georgia, gospel station. That only gave Wayne the idea of singing along with the songs that played:

"*I'm giving my life up to Jee-zus / I'm giving my life to the Lor-r-rd . . .*"

At that point, his father had heard enough. Wayne's singing was terrible. It sounded as if he were making fun of the songs more than singing them with sincerity. Annoyed, his father turned to look back into his son's eyes. He shouted, "Wayne! What in the world is your . . ."

Before Mr. Ellerbee could finish his sentence, a car smashed into the driver's side of their minivan.

BOOM!

"AAAAHHHHH!" Mrs. Ellerbee and the kids screamed.

"DAD-DEEE!" Cynthia yelled.

"BAY-BEEE, ARE YOU OKAY?" Mrs. Ellerbee screamed to her husband in the brief silence after the impact. "ARE

YOU KIDS ALL RIGHT?" she screamed to her children in the back.

"WHAT HAPPENED?" Wayne shouted.

The impact of the crash knocked the Ellerbee family into a parking meter at the curb, shattered their front windshield, and deployed both of their front air bags. Everyone seemed fine except for their father. Mr. Ellerbee was bleeding from a cut on his forehead and was slumped back in his driver's seat.

"Call the ambulance," he mumbled softly.

His wife asked him, "Do you feel anything broken?"

Mr. Ellerbee paused and remained still. "I can't tell," he answered.

Mrs. Ellerbee was already on her cell phone calling 9-1-1. "Yes, I need to report an accident at the intersection of . . ." She looked to make sure she had the correct streets, "Peachtree and Tenth Street."

Then she listened as the operator responded to her.

"Yes, we do need an emergency ambulance," she stated. "My husband is injured."

Wayne and the kids were still in shock as they unbuckled their seatbelts and climbed out of the sliding door to reach the sidewalk. Their mother remained inside the minivan with their father.

"Jesus, are you kids all right?" the driver of the other car asked Wayne, Cynthia and Dalvin on the sidewalk.

He was a balding, middle-aged man, who wore a Sunday suit himself that morning.

"Yeah, we're fine, but my father's not," Wayne told him.

In fact, Wayne had never seen his father that helpless before, and it scared him. His sister and brother were already crying as they looked in on their injured father and watched the cars that drove past the accident.

The man at fault then approached their mother in the passenger side of the minivan.

"Is he all right?" he asked of her husband.

"I'm not sure yet, but we'll wait for the ambulance before we try and move him anywhere," Mrs. Ellerbee commented.

After she ended her phone call to the police operator, the man took out his license and insurance card to hand over to her. "I'm ah, terribly sorry about this. The wheel just got away from me for a second."

"And a split second is all it takes most of the time," Mrs. Ellerbee responded. She took down the man's information and gave him theirs.

Wayne watched everything from the sidewalk with nervous anxiety, praying that his father would be okay. He wondered *If I had never started singing, maybe they wouldn't have had an accident. Maybe Dad would have seen the car before it hit them. Or maybe the car would have hit them anyway.*

When the police arrived at the scene, followed by the emergency ambulance, Wayne watched and listened carefully as the medics pulled out a stretcher and eased his father out from behind the wheel. That made Cynthia and Dalvin cry even louder.

"Is Daddy okay, Mom?" his sister asked.

Mrs. Ellerbee hugged her daughter and youngest son

close to her. "Yes, baby, he'll be okay. They're all just making sure, that's all."

Wayne wondered if his mother had left him out of the hug on purpose. Did she feel that he was to blame for their accident? Maybe his mother did feel that way. That made Wayne feel sad.

Mrs. Ellerbee explained the accident to the police. "The driver of the car overran the median and hit us on the front driver's side. He said he lost control of the wheel."

Wayne listened to his mother's explanation as the police took down notes. He started to think, *It's all my fault. It's all my fault.*

By the time they all climbed into the ambulance, where their father had been transferred to a gurney, tears began to swell up in Wayne's eyes. His father was stretched out on his back with tubes running into his arms, and the medics continued to test him for various injuries.

"So, you're feeling pain in your neck, your back, and in your chest area, is that right?" they asked him.

"Yes," his dad answered them softly.

Wayne could not even look his family members in their eyes anymore. He felt very guilty. *What if my father can never walk again?* he thought. Fresh tears began to roll down his face.

Finally, his mother looked over to him. She could read the grief on her son's face. So she held his hand and said, "It's not your fault, Wayne. Things just happen like that sometimes."

Wayne mumbled, "But if I hadn't made Daddy mad . . ."

Mrs. Ellerbee squeezed her son's hand and said, "Wayne,

if that car was gonna hit us, it was gonna hit us. There was nothing you could do about it."

Wayne listened to his mother's explanation, but he still didn't agree with it. His father had deliberately turned away from the wheel to respond to his mockery-filled singing of the gospel song.

I just need to grow up and stop being so stupid! Wayne told himself. He was getting harder on himself by the minute.

Once his family reached the nearest Atlanta hospital, the ambulance pulled up to the emergency room entrance. They all climbed out the back before the medics wheeled their father's gurney onto a lowering ramp and out of the ambulance toward the opening emergency doors.

Mrs. Ellerbee and her children followed the medics through the hospital hallways and into the awaiting examination room, where a gray-bearded doctor appeared to see him.

The doctor looked at the concerned family members and asked Mrs. Ellerbee, "Would the children like to wait in the waiting room, or would you like them to remain here?"

Mrs. Ellerbee looked at Wayne immediately and thought it over. She was unsure whether her oldest son had the maturity to watch his younger sister and brother alone. Wayne could rarely be trusted with much responsibility.

"Well, are we in the way?" Mrs. Ellerbee asked the doctor.

The doctor shook his head. "No, not at all. I just wanted to ask first to make sure. Some kids don't like the emergency room much. Then again, other kids can deal with it."

Mrs. Ellerbee continued to think it over. Finally, Mr. Ellerbee spoke up from his bed.

"Honey, let Wayne go out there and watch his brother and sister."

She stared at her husband to make sure. Instead of voicing his approval, Mr. Ellerbee tried to nod to her, only to feel a sharp pain in his injured neck.

"Ahh," he groaned.

With that, the doctor cautioned his patient, "Try not to make any sudden movements, sir."

"Relax, honey," his wife told him with a delicate hand on his arm.

Mr. Ellerbee took a breath and composed himself. Then he lifted his left hand and mumbled, "Wayne . . . come here."

Wayne stepped over to the bed, feeling nervous. What would his father say to him? He answered, "Yes, Dad."

His father reached out his hand to him. Wayne took his hand in his, still feeling anxious.

I'm sorry, Dad. It was all my fault, he wanted to tell his father.

His father told him slowly, "Now, I know that you don't like being the oldest child in the house, and you don't like having such a big burden on your shoulders. But the fact is, you *are* the oldest, and as a young man, you have to learn how to accept your position in this family, just like I do, and your mother, and your sister and brother whenever the burden of responsibility falls on them.

"You understand me now?" his father asked him. "Because the Lord is telling me that I may not be able to walk that road with you. My yelling and screaming and whipping you are not gonna be the answer. You have to grow up on your own terms."

Wayne thought about everything that happened that morning, and he did understand. He would be the oldest Ellerbee child regardless of how he felt about it. So he nodded his head and responded, "Yes, Dad. I understand."

"Good," his father told him. "Now you need to go on out there and sit inside the waiting room with your brother and sister so your mother and I can talk to the doctor alone."

Wayne nodded and said, "Okay."

"And son," his father told him, "I love you."

"I love you too, Dad."

When Wayne turned to lead his younger brother and sister out of the room, the gray-bearded doctor nodded to him and shook his hand.

"Your father's gonna be just fine, Wayne. I'm gonna make sure of that for ya'. All right?"

Wayne cracked a reluctant smile and said, "All right." Then his younger siblings followed him out of the room.

The waiting room was a wide open space with plenty of chairs and a color television. Wayne felt proud of having a new opportunity to be a big brother. His parents were counting on him, and he didn't want to let them down again. He found three empty chairs in the room and sat down between his brother and sister.

He looked Dalvin in the eyes and asked him, "Are you okay?"

His brother nodded. "Yeah," he answered slowly.

Wayne then looked into Cynthia's eyes. "Are you okay?"

She shook her head no. "I'm scared," she told him.

Wayne reached out and held her hand. He said, "The doctor told us he'll be okay. Did you hear him say that?"

His sister nodded. "Yeah, I heard him, but I'm still scared."

Wayne didn't know what else to say, so he hugged his sister instead. "He'll be all right," he comforted. "He just may have to stay in the hospital to get better for a couple of days, that's all."

Dalvin heard that and became alarmed.

"Stay in the hospital?" he responded. "But Daddy has to go to work."

"Not if he's hurt, he doesn't," Cynthia spoke up. "All he has to do is tell his boss that he was in a accident."

"But how many days will he have to stay here?" Dalvin asked.

Wayne answered, "Mom'll probably tell us when she comes back out."

An older woman watched them from her chair across the room and was impressed with how well Wayne handled the situation. When he looked in her direction, she gave him a proud smile and a nod.

A few minutes later, after they had all calmed down and started watching television, their mother walked out of the emergency room with the updated news on their father's injuries.

She sat down next to her wide-eyed children and said, "Okay guys, Daddy's going to be okay, but the doctor said it's best for him to remain in the hospital for a few days. He has to take pain medicine and heal his injuries a little bit first. Okay? And then we'll all come back to pick him up on Tuesday evening."

Wayne smiled and told his sister and brother, "You see that? That's just what I told you before Mom did."

They both nodded and agreed.

"So, how do we get to church or back home now with no car?" Cynthia asked their mother.

Mrs. Ellerbee answered, "Well, we're not gonna go to church now, honey. We'll all just go home now and pray for Daddy. And we'll take a taxi home."

———

On the ride home from the hospital, Mrs. Ellerbee sat up front, and the children sat in the back of the taxi together, holding hands. Wayne never liked holding hands with his sister and brother before, but on this Sunday he did. He wanted them to know that he really cared about them.

When they arrived home, the Ellerbee family all sat together at the kitchen table and prayed for their father. Later, instead of separating from his family for his own activities as usual, Wayne decided to read books to his sister and brother and help his mother out in the kitchen. She had begun to prepare an early dinner.

And for the next two days, Wayne Ellerbee became the perfect older brother at home. He helped everyone clean their rooms. He helped get his sister and brother breakfast in the morning without them having to beg him. He helped gather the dirty laundry to take down to the family laundry room. He helped to collect and empty out all of the trash cans in the house. And he forced himself to get out of bed earlier, wash his face and brush his teeth without being pushed to do so. Wayne was determined not to let his father down while he recovered in the hospital.

Dad is counting on me to be the man of the house now, he told himself.

When they all went to pick their father up from the hospital on Tuesday evening, Mrs. Ellerbee told her husband all about Wayne's miraculous change. She was so pleased that she had saved the surprise for her husband so she could tell him in person instead of over the phone. She knew that it would mean a lot more to Wayne if he could see how his father responded to the good news.

Sure enough, his dad smiled from ear to ear, as he sat in the passenger seat of their rented minivan. Mr. Ellerbee was wearing a soft brace to support his neck.

"Is that right?" he asked his wife. Then he asked his younger children about it. "So guys, Wayne has been a great big brother?"

Cynthia and Dalvin both smiled. "Yes," they answered in unison.

Mr. Ellerbee looked at his oldest son and smiled. He had tears in his eyes, and was filled with gratitude. He said, "I'm proud of you, son. I knew you could do it."

He looked over at the rest of his family and added, "I'm proud of *all* of you. And I love you all."

They all smiled back at their dad.

Wayne told him, "The doctor promised us you would be

all right. Now he says you only have to wear your neck brace for a couple days to strengthen your neck while you take the pain medicine."

Mr. Ellerbee grinned and said, "That's right. And it sounds like you were paying him strict attention."

"I was," Wayne told him. "Like I'm a *mini* doctor," he joked. They all shared a laugh at Wayne's good humor.

"Well, all right, little doc. You help me to pull it back together then," his dad responded with a chuckle.

Wayne helped his father out of the van and helped him as he gingerly walked him back to the house. They all returned home with happy smiles on their faces. They were glad to have their father back with them, and Wayne was now pleased to be the big brother.

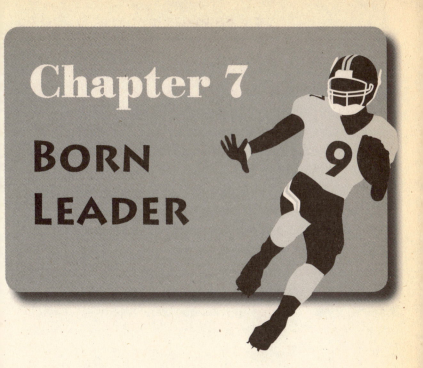

Chapter 7

BORN LEADER

"We're almost at the top," Alfred shouted, hurrying up the mountainside. He climbed over small rocks as he followed the much treaded pathway of Mount Pocono. He yelled back with enthusiasm to his 12-year-old buddy, Adrian, who was exhausted just trying to keep up with him.

"It's about time," Adrian huffed, more than 10 yards behind him.

They both wore the red T-shirts of Camp Shango. It was their last Saturday of a two-week stay in the mountainside camp of Pennsylvania. Alfred had waited patiently, through all the other events that they had since early July, to climb Mount Pocono again. Climbing the mountain had possessed his young, courageous mind. It was his favorite part of going to camp there, and Alfred was determined to beat his previous climbing times.

"Quit pouting, and come on," Alfred yelled back as he continued climbing the mountain in a furry, ahead of his friend. The clear blue sky looked more beautiful as they got closer to the top. It even looked reachable.

"Wow! They're all the way back there," Adrian said, giggling as he looked down the mountainside at the rest of the campers. He and Alfred had climbed ahead of them long ago. The other campers struggled to make it up the long, steep trail, like an army of bright red ants, marching up the side of a giant green cupcake.

"I know," Alfred agreed, looking back with a smile. His small, 12-year-old, muscular brown frame was juiced with energy. "Come on, man. We almost caught up to Mr. Steve."

Adrian was the same height and build as Alfred, with the same amount of boundless energy. He just wasn't as excited as Alfred was to make it up Mount Pocono in record time.

"We're not gonna catch Mr. Steve," he argued, speeding up his pace a bit. The small pebbles and rocks rolled under his red, black and white Jordan basketball shoes as he climbed.

"Yes, we can. He's right in front of us," Alfred assured him.

Soon they had both caught up to Mr. Steve, a 19-year-old junior counselor, who had slowed down his pace after realizing the annual Camp Shango mountain climb was almost over.

"Wow! You guys left everybody," he said, stopping to wait for them. Mr. Steve was tall, brown and skinny, wore sunglasses and a red, Camp Shango baseball cap to match his red T-shirt. He had his baseball cap turned to the back.

"Are we almost there?" Alfred asked him to make sure.

"Yeah, we have just another hundred feet or so," Mr. Steve answered. He stepped to the right of the path to take out his Army-camouflaged canteen for a drink of water. "You want some?" he offered them both.

"Naw, man. I don't want to drink anything until I get to the top," Alfred responded before Adrian could. He then started to climb again.

"I want some," Adrian answered, stopping with Mr. Steve. Mr. Steve gave him the canteen and quickly looked up to Alfred.

"HOLD ON, ALFRED! A counselor has to be in front of you," he yelled.

"WELL COME ON THEN," Alfred yelled back, still climbing ahead. Adrian looked at Mr. Steve and laughed.

"That boy is something else," he said, taking another drink from the canteen.

"Well, come on. Let's catch up to him," Mr. Steve said. He knew the camp regulations. He was a 10-year Camp Shango veteran, and he had been climbing Mount Pocono since he was a young camper there himself.

"HOLD ON, ALFRED!" he yelled again, nervous that Alfred would beat him up to the top. Alfred was only 50 feet away from it, and he kept moving right ahead.

"That boy's gonna get me in hot water," Mr. Steve said, chuckling to Adrian, who was right behind him.

"That's the way he is, Mr. Steve. Alfred always wants be first," Adrian responded, chuckling to himself. Mr. Steve then took off his sunglasses, put them in his back shorts pocket, and jetted up the mountainside to catch Alfred before the young camper beat him.

Mr. Steve moved like a man on fire, half out of fear and half out of athletic competition. But it didn't matter. Alfred still beat him by 10 feet.

"Ha ha ha! I see Alfred beat you up," Mr. Carlton commented with a laugh. He was a senior counselor who had driven up the mountaintop in the camp van. He and several other staff members had lunches and drinks ready when the hungry campers arrived. He saw Steve dash from the mountain pathway shortly after Alfred, as if a grizzly bear was chasing him.

Mr. Carlton chuckled and continued. "Yup, Alfred just set a new, Camp Shango record for junior camp." He was a round-bellied man with a short, fuzzy afro and glasses. He was holding a stop watch in hand.

"My stop watch says 40 minutes and 12 seconds," he announced. "The senior camp is only doing 37 minutes. So Alfred must have really been moving." He grabbed Alfred by the shoulders as Steve smiled and doubled over to catch his breath.

Mr. Carlton nodded and said, "Well, congratulations, Alfred. But next time just make sure you don't stray too far in front of the counselor."

Alfred smiled and agreed to it, while Mr. Steve continued to catch his breath, followed by Adrian, who had just reached the top.

That night Alfred received more awards at the annual Camp Shango Award Ceremony. He had been receiving awards at Camp Shango every year since he was nine. But he was now 12 and would be graduating to senior camp for the 13- to 16-year-olds next year. He smiled and said a short, "Thank you" at the podium. Everyone talked about him that night, referring to all the awards that he had won in swimming, track, archery, canoeing and basketball.

Because of Alfred, the Mandingoes, his 15-member cabin unit, beat the Zulus, the Egyptians, and the Nubians in their various competitive events during War Day. The Mandingoes tallied the most points. Alfred even won awards for African Cultural Studies by memorizing and reciting the most historic facts about African people and culture.

———

In late September, Alfred was back with 31 students inside a noisy classroom in Trenton, New Jersey, daydreaming. He was thinking about Saturday's upcoming football game, where he would play quarterback on offense, free safety on defense, the kicker on the kick-off team and the return man on the receiving team. He had led his Wildcats team to a 3-0 record, with a 27-point margin of victory for each game. Alfred had thrown for nine touchdowns and run for six. And so far that season, he was the most talked about player in the 95-pound weight class in the city's Police Athletic League. But school was a different story.

More than a few teachers had gotten used to telling Alfred to put his hand down instead of allowing him to try to answer all of their classroom discussion questions. So Alfred got bored and started to daydream.

"It ain't my fault they're slow," he would state, referring to the other seventh-grade students. Few classmates dared to challenge him because Alfred was used to winning his fights too.

"Alfred Jenkins? Did you read the three paragraphs that I assigned?" Mrs. Payton drilled him. Mrs. Payton was old, gray and wise. She had been teaching in the Trenton Public School system for more than 25 years.

"Yeah," Alfred answered with an attitude.

"Well then, read it aloud for the rest of the class," she urged. She had dealt with Alfred's type before and realized that some students needed the extra challenge. Alfred would perform best that way.

"Hee, hee, hee," a female classmate to his right giggled.

Alfred eyed her sternly and said, "At least I can *read*."

"So, I can read too," she retorted, sucking her teeth.

"Mitchell, leave Alfred alone," Mrs. Payton interjected.

"But I didn't even say anything to him," Mitchell whined, shaking her cornrowed head. She faced Mrs. Payton, who was at her desk, three seats from where Mitchell and Alfred sat in the classroom.

"You shouldn't have been laughing at me," Alfred snapped back to her. He was pleased that Mrs. Payton seemed to be on his side for a change.

"Whatever, boy," Mitchell commented, rolling her eyes at him. She was as boisterous and as energetic as Alfred could be. She liked him too. She just didn't know any other way to express it, other than teasing him.

"They're always arguing," a girl sitting in the front seat stated.

"Won't you mind your *business*, Kimberly," Mitchell warned her, rolling her eyes at Kimberly. Mrs. Payton gave her an evil eye, and Mitchell finally got the picture. With one more word she would have gotten a detention after school.

"Alfred, go ahead and read the paragraphs, please," Mrs. Payton told him, redirecting her class. She had dealt with many of Mitchell's type before too. She knew that it was an expression of young puppy love on the girl's part, but she had a class to teach.

"In 1492, Christopher Columbus became the first to discover America," Alfred began. But then he stopped right there. He said, "At my summer camp, we learned that Africans from Mali, Egypt and the Congo had come to America way before Columbus." Then Alred waited for Mrs. Payton to disagree with him so that he could argue his point with her. In fact, he was ready for it, and the rest of his classmates listened to see if he was correct. However, the bell rang before Mrs. Payton got a chance to respond to him.

"Hold on, Alfred," she called to him, while the other students scrambled out the door for their next period. Mitchell waited too, curious to see what Mrs. Payton was going to say.

Mrs. Payton walked near the door where Alfred stood. She smiled at him, a warm and proud smile. "We need to rewrite these books one day," she told him. She held up the textbook. The cover displayed three White drummer-boys carrying an American flag. She put her aging hand on Alfred's shoulder. "Who knows? Maybe you'll be one to help us to do it."

Mitchell looked on, convinced that she was pursuing a good catch for a boyfriend.

"I thought you was gonna say that I was wrong," Alfred admitted, feeling relieved by his teacher's response.

"N-o-o-o-o, young man. We colored folks have been talking for years about rewriting history to include *all* of the real facts about our accomplishments," she said, continuing to smile. "But I'm too old now to help do it," she admitted. She walked out the door with Alfred and Mitchell following her.

"My mom said that my hairstyle is African," Mitchell announced, feeling proud about it now. She didn't much like her cornrows before. "But were we here first, Mrs. Payton?" Mitchell wanted to know for sure.

"Not all of us, just some earlier voyagers from Africa to South America," Alfred interjected. "Most of us didn't come to North America until the slave trades. But a lot of Black people were indentured servants first," he added.

Mrs. Payton was impressed. Mitchell looked at her teacher again to see if what Alfred said was correct. But Mrs. Payton wasn't quite sure herself. "It's a shame how they have done us," she said. She was slightly embarrassed that she had been a teacher for so many years, and yet she was still not too sure about African-American history. And Alfred was only 12.

"Alfred, I have the perfect teacher for you to meet on Monday," Mrs. Payton blurted out, inspired by their conversation. She captured Alfred's full attention. "She's a new, young teacher with an African name. Aminah," Mrs. Payton informed him.

"Okay," Alfred said. He was surprised at how enthusiastic his usually reserved teacher had become.

"Well, I'll tell her about you today when I see her during our lunch break," she told him, putting her hand on his shoulder again.

Alfred and Mitchell then headed in the opposite direction from Mrs. Payton.

"What do you want to be, Alfred?" Mitchell was curious to know. After witnessing how pleased he had just made "grouchy Mrs. Payton," Mitchell scooted up beside him as they walked.

"I'm gonna be the president," Alfred said sarcastically, before he laughed.

"For real?" Mitchell responded, believing him.

"No, girl. I don't know." He was annoyed that she didn't catch his joke.

"Well, I'm gonna be a track star and a model," she said back, holding her head up high.

"Nobody wants to look at you," Alfred teased, facing her.

"How you know?" Mitchell asked him.

"Never mind," Alfred responded, heading away from her.

"You're gonna play football at recess again?" Mitchell called after him. Alfred and his friends played football nearly everyday at recess.

"No, I have a game tomorrow," he answered. "So I have to save my arm." He vowed to never play at recess on Fridays until football season was over.

Alfred headed home after school, thinking about nothing but tomorrow's football game. The Wildcats were playing the Saints, and the Saints were undefeated in three games as well.

"AY ALFRED, YOUR BROTHER JUST GOT LOCKED UP!" a young neighbor shouted from his window as soon as Alfred reached his home.

"For what?" Alfred said nonchalantly. He was just walking up to the front steps of his house and toward the broken screen door. All three of his older brothers had been arrested or in trouble with the law before. So it was no longer a big deal to Alfred.

"I don't know. The cops just grabbed him, pushed him up against a car and started slamming him around."

Alfred shook his head with no comment. And he walked into his house without a word.

"I knew that boy was gonna get caught stealing sooner or later," his mother was saying, making a phone call. She didn't pay Alfred any mind when he walked in. He was surprised to even see his mother at home. She usually worked until seven at night, and didn't arrive home until almost eight.

"Yes, is Wallace Hobbs in, please?" she asked. Alfred smiled, knowing that whenever his mother made sure to sound articulate, there was a professional White person on the other end of the line. "Hi, this is Marvene Jenkins. Remember me, with the four sons? I'm terribly sorry to have to bother you like this, but my second son was just arrested, and I didn't want to go down there to the precinct without having legal advice. I know they will start asking me about his previous record and things," she said, all in one breath.

Then she nodded her head, listening. "Mmm hmm," she mumbled several times before speaking.

Finally, she said, "Okay then, well, I thank you so much, Mr. Hobbs . . . I mean Wallace," she said, correcting herself. Wallace Hobbs had always reminded her to call him Wallace, but she liked to refer to him as Mr. Hobbs. To her, it made their relationship sound more professional.

"Darn it, that boy lucky I was home. But I'm *sick* of this, Alfred. I'm just *sick* of it!" his mother faced Alfred and spoke her words sternly. She then gave him the evil eye as if *he* had done something wrong.

"What did *I* do?" Alfred asked her innocently.

"Nothing yet, but don't you get involved in these streets like your brothers, you hear me? It ain't nothin' out there for you but trouble," she said, standing up from the brand new, living room couch. She shook off her shoes, put her hand to her forehead and started shaking her head in despair. "Jesus, help me. I just wish that we could move away from this place. I tries so hard to give these kids all a good home, but these darn streets just take them away from me."

Alfred walked away from his mother's praying and went up to his room. He didn't feel like being bothered with his mother's street preaching. She could go on and on about the streets, how their father had died, and how you can't find a good man who wants a woman with *four* "hard headed" sons.

Lester, the oldest, was a 19-year-old, high school drop out. Peanut, who had just gotten arrested, was a 16-year-old hoodlum, trying hard to break into anything illegal. And Walter, the third son, was 15 and "lazy as he wanna be," his mother always said about him. But Alfred was humbled and was reminded by his mother daily to stay on track. She kept him busy playing football, basketball, baseball and continuing in his school work. Alfred didn't have much of a choice. It's was either stay busy, positive and motivated, or face the negativity of the street life like his brothers.

"I don't care what my brothers do. I'm gonna make it," Alfred would often repeat to himself. So he remained determined to push himself to succeed.

———

"ARE Y'ALL FIRED UP?"

"YES, SIR."

"ARE Y'ALL FIRED UP?"

"YES, SIR."

"WHO ARE WE?"

"THE WILDCATS."

"WHO ARE WE?"

"THE WILDCATS."

Alfred and his Wildcats teammates football team ran their warm-up laps that Saturday morning in their black and gold uniforms. Their black face guards matched the two black stripes across their shiny, sunlight-reflecting gold helmets. Alfred's teammates were fired up on a sunny day perfect for football. The visiting Saints won the coin toss to receive the ball first. And after the first half had ended, the score was still tied at zero, as all the mothers, fathers, family and friends watched a hard-hitting, defensive ball-game.

"Man, them boys are hitting hard," one of Alfred's teammate commented. At halftime they all headed over to their side of the field.

"What did you say, Forsett?" one of the assistant coaches asked sternly. "Give me 25 push ups." He said, "They're not hitting any harder than we are. We just gotta put some points on the board out there."

Forsett did his push-ups and got back to his feet, exhausted.

"Jenkins, we gotta start putting the ball in the air on these boys," the offensive coach advised Alfred.

"Yeah, but I can't get enough time to throw. Every time I drop back, they come right through the line. I can't even see," Alfred explained, as he took off his helmet.

"That's because we're not blocking up on the line," the head coach interjected. He was usually calm during their wins, but this was the first time the team was not ahead by at least two touchdowns.

"What's wrong with you guys today? These kids took your heart or what?" he asked his team of 11- and 12-year-olds. They were all inner-city youth coated in various shades of brown skin. The Saints had a multicultural team from the New Jersey suburbs.

"Man, those guys playing dirty. 'Cause they grabbing your jerseys and throwing dirt and stuff," another teammate complained.

"I know. That's why I was about to fight number 42. But I got him good though."

"Listen to you," the head coach told them. "You all over

here so busy talking about what *they're* doing, that they've taken you right out of your ball game. Now what we need to do is get back out there and get the job done. *They're* three-and-oh and *we're* three-and-oh. And when this ball game is over with, only one team will be left undefeated. Now who is that gonna be?"

"Us!" Alfred spoke up confidently.

The coach said, "Well, let's get back out there and do it then. Talk is cheap."

The team headed back on to the field for halftime warm-ups, and the head coach pulled Alfred over to the sideline.

"Now Alfred, since they're rushing right in on you, you can probably get some quarterback sneaks in. So we're gonna start off with the passing game, and then we're gonna let you run it right up the middle on them. All right?" the coach explained.

"All right," Alfred responded, fastening his chin-strap.

Alfred received the second half kick-off from the Saints and took off running up the right side of the field. He cut back toward the middle as the defense over-pursued. And with more speed than anyone on the field, Alfred outran them all, sprinting 76 yards for the first touchdown of the game.

"JESUS CHRIST, TOMMY! I TOLD YOU NEVER TO LEAVE YOUR SIDE OF THE FIELD! HOW MANY TIMES DO WE HAVE TO GO OVER THESE SAME KICK-OFF DRILLS!" the Saints defensive coach screamed to one of the players. He even grabbed his player off the field by his jersey.

"Yeah, Alfred, them boys ain't nothin'! We can beat them!" a teammate ran into the end zone and shouted hysterically. They all crowded around their quarterback after the long score.

The Wildcats failed to score the extra point, and neither team could move the ball for the rest of game. Alfred couldn't even sneak a running play up the middle. The Saints defense was too good. The game ended 6-0. The Wildcats increased their record to 4-0.

Alfred arrived at home, took a quick shower, changed into clean clothes, and went out to celebrate the victory with pizza. The coaches were treating.

"Alfred, you pulled that game out of the hat for us," the assistant coach said. Everyone was enjoying their victory celebration at Pizza Hut. And Alfred smiled with a stuffed mouth as they all fed him more ego-boosting compliments.

"Alfred returned that kick-off like a torpedo," one of the coaches commented.

"Yeah, he was like lightning in the sunshine," said another coach.

Alfred said, "It was nothing, Coach Smith. I just saw daylight to the left, and I took off running."

"Yeah, you sure did," his teammates told him. "And no one else could even score."

———

"Alfred Jenkins, this is Mrs. Aminah Dali," a happy-faced Mrs. Payton announced that Monday morning at school. It was lunch break and she had gotten Alfred to follow her to the teacher's lounge.

"Well, how are you, *Bomani*?" Mrs. Dali asked Alfred. She wore Kente clothing and a tiny, gold loop earring in her nose. She was light-brown, tall and slender.

"How you know I was a warrior?" Alfred asked. He had learned the meaning of several African Swahili names at Camp Shango.

Mrs. Dali stood from her seat. She was eating a healthy salad. She answered, "Because I've already heard about you," and shook his firm hand. Alfred was looking up at her, impressed with her strong personality, looks and tall stature.

Mrs. Payton said, "Yes, and I wanted you two to meet, because Alfred seems to know a lot about Africa. And I don't want to steer him wrong."

Mrs. Dali put her right hand to her lip and pondered for a moment, while Alfred continued to admire her. She asked him, "How would you like to join my husband's, 'Rights of Passage' class? He usually deals with older, teenaged boys who've been in trouble with the system, but I don't see why *you* can't participate. We don't always have to wait for someone to get in trouble first."

"Yeah, we learned about 'Rights of Passage' at summer camp," Alfred told her excitedly. He would be delighted to join. He saw it as a privilege.

"Well, they meet on Sundays inside my basement at 12 noon. Do you go to church on Sundays?" Mrs. Dali asked him. She wanted to make sure that the day and time would not conflict.

"Unt unh," Alfred said distastefully. He shook his head. He thought church was for old people and kids who sing in the choir.

Mrs. Payton told him, "Church is good for a young soul."

Mrs. Dali smiled. She said, "Every person finds their own way to truth and knowledge eventually." Then she started to write down her husband's name, their phone number, and their address on a piece of note pad paper.

"What's your parents' names and phone number?" she asked Alfred after giving him the note-pad paper with her information on it.

"My mom's name is Marvene, but my father died four years ago in a car crash," Alfred informed her solemnly.

Mrs. Dali paused. She said, "Oh . . . well, I'm sorry to hear that."

"It's okay," he told her.

Mrs. Payton nodded her head with concern. She didn't know much about Alfred's family. But with no father figure, it seemed even more important to link him up with good role models.

"Do you have any brothers and sisters?" Mrs. Dali asked him.

"Yeah, I got three older brothers," Alfred answered. "And they've all been in plenty of trouble." He figured there was no sense in him lying about it. His older brothers needed more guidance than he did.

"Oh, so you're the baby," Mrs. Dali commented. "Well, what I'm going to do is call your mother and explain what my husband's program is all about. Okay?" she told him.

She was committed to getting involved in helping the young man to keep a focused path. He seemed filled with so much enthusiasm and potential.

Alfred nodded to her, feeling good about it. "Okay," he agreed.

"All right, well, I'll get your mother's phone number and information from Mrs. Payton, and I'll be talking to you," Mrs. Dali informed him, shaking Alfred's hand again before he left them.

Mrs. Payton sat down at the teachers' lunch table and took out a sandwich and salad as her inspiring sixth grade student walked off to enjoy his recess.

"That boy has bundles of energy and talent," she told Ms. Dali. "There needs to be advanced classes for students like him, because he gets so bored and distracted when the work isn't challenging him enough. But there's only so much you can do when you have thirty other children to teach."

"And some of the brighter ones end up getting lost in the shuffle," Mrs. Dali agreed. "That's what happens to a lot of our bright boys. But in the 'Rights of Passage' instruction, the young Black males are put into kin groups where they lead or follow according to their own pace and temperaments. Alfred is definitely a leader, but he doesn't get the chance to lead in the classroom. So students like him tend to turn to sports or street gangs to display their leadership skills. That's where my husband and I come in—to make sure that they have other outlets that are available to them."

Mrs. Payton sat there and grinned at the younger teacher, while taking the first bite of her sandwich. She was amazed by what she had not learned in all of her years of teaching. She had never taken any courses in African culture, and she was 52 years old.

———

Mrs. Dali called Marvene Jenkins that night and explained her husband's Rights of Passage program. Marvene immediately became intrigued by it. She thought the program was exactly what her youngest son needed to help him stay out of trouble and stay on the right track. So all that week, Alfred eagerly anticipated meeting Dr. Barry Dali, the well-respected instructor of African and African-American history at Rutgers University.

When Sunday had finally arrived, Alfred found himself at the Dali family's doorsteps. Feeling both nervous and excited, he rang the front doorbell.

"Well, hello, *Bomani*. Come on in," Mrs. Dali greeted him.

Their house had a warm scent of nature to it, like herbal tea. It was bright and colorful with African art placed around its shiny wooden floors, and African-American paintings hanging on their off-white painted walls. Alfred found himself floating in the comfort of their spacious home.

"Hi," a little one decked out in blue, gold and white Kente cloth spoke to him. Alfred looked at the small boy and saw an immediate resemblance to Mrs. Dali.

"What's up?" Alfred said back, shaking the little one's hand.

Mrs. Dali smiled. "Alfred, this is my son, Kofi. Kofi, this is Alfred Jenkins. Now Kofi, take Alfred downstairs to meet everyone," she told her son as she headed back to the kitchen.

"She making cookies," Kofi informed Alfred, before he led him to the basement stairs.

Alfred walked down the basement steps, eyeing more African artifacts that hung from the walls. When they reached the bottom of the stairs, Kofi ran into the middle of a group of eight boys. They were sitting on small cushions with their legs crossed, all wearing colorful Kente cloth.

"*Habari gani*?" asked Dr. Barry Dali, speaking the Swahili greeting for "how are you." Dr. Dali sat at the center of the young men's circle. He smiled, projecting warmth and confidence. He had a healthy brown face, wide eyes, and a neatly trimmed beard and mustache.

"*Seju, bebe,*" Alfred answered back in Swahili meaning "fine, and you?" Then he noticed an empty cushion on the far end of the circle.

Dr. Dali extended a hand to Alfred pointing to the empty cushion. "Have a seat, my brother. We've all been waiting to meet you," he commenting, switching back to English. The other boys began to smile and nod to him with their greetings.

"*Habari gani*?"

Alfred felt proud, not knowing what he would learn or what they would all do. But he loved the experience of introducing himself to a new membership of friends. *Who knows where it all would lead?* Alfred thought. Alfred just hoped his new membership would produce good things. He only wished that some of his teammates and his brothers could join them as well and feel all that he felt.

A larger Rights of Passage group would prepare them all for the daily challenges of the world as young Black warriors. So Alfred took a seat. He began to think about ways he could lead others to enjoy the same teachings that he would receive from his knowledgeable elders. And he knew that teaching through experience would become his mission.

Chapter 8

BLACK, LIKE ME

"I'm Cannonball from the New Mutants," Dean told his group of four friends. They were all inside his basement leaning over Dean's *Marvel Universe Encyclopedia*, discussing their favorite comic book heroes.

"That's the one who turns into a rocket, right?" Alexander asked him, while flipping through the book. "I like the Silver Surfer."

"Yeah, you're long and skinny like the Silver Surfer too," Sean commented. "And Dean looks just like Cannonball. He has blonde hair and blue eyes just like him."

Sean had light brown hair and green eyes. His hair was a shade lighter than Alexander's dark brown hair. Alexander also had dark brown eyes.

"Who's your favorite superhero?" Alexander asked Sean.

"I just like Spiderman," Sean answered. "He has the coolest powers. And I like the Hulk too."

"Those are like, everybody's favorites," Dean responded.

"No, my favorite hero is Iron Man. I like him because he's a rich scientist," responded Emilio. He was a Latino kid with black hair and dark eyes.

"Yeah, his red and yellow armor suit is pretty cool," Sean told him.

Once the rest of the boys had revealed their favorite superheroes, Jamal expected them to ask who his favorites were. It was only a matter of time.

"What about you, Jamal? Who's your favorite hero?" Dean asked him.

Jamal was the only African-American kid in the room, and one of the few in their sixth grade class. He had smooth dark brown skin and a short afro of tight curls. But he hesitated before he answered. What if they didn't like his favorite?

"Umm . . . I like the Black Panther."

There was a moment of silence in the room.

Alexander was the first to speak. He said, "The Black Panther?" he asked. "What powers does he have?"

Emilio grabbed the *Marvel Universe Encyclopedia* from the floor and flipped the pages to the B section to look up the Black Panther.

"Here he is. It says he's an Olympic athlete, acrobat, gymnast and combat specialist," Emilio read. "And he has a mask that enhances his night vision. He has gloves that expel gases. It says he has boots that let him jump and land from great heights. And his vibranium costume makes bullets or punches lose power."

"Whoa, let me see that guy," Sean said. They all moved toward the book to get a better look at Jamal's favorite hero.

"Hey, he looks a little bit like Batman," Dean commented while eyeing the picture of Black Panther in the book.

"Yeah, but Batman has a lot more gadgets and stuff," Alexander said.

"Who do you think would win in a fight between the Black Panther and Batman, Jamal?" Emilio asked him.

Jamal was at a loss for words. He was surprised they were spending that much time on his favorite hero in the first place. They hadn't looked up anyone else's favorite hero in the book.

"I don't know," Jamal answered shyly.

"Well, how'd you find out about him?" Sean asked him. "It says he's a king or something."

Jamal nodded to him. He said, "Yeah, he's the king of Wakanda in Africa. My uncle has his comics, so I started reading them because of him."

Alexander read the information in the book as well. He added, "It says he married Storm from the X-Men."

Jamal began to smile. He said, "Yeah, they have a new comic out about the Black Panther and Storm now. I have them all at home."

Sean nodded and said, "Oh, yeah, I did see that comic. They had it at the book store. I just didn't know who he was."

"Well, now you do," Jamal told him.

Dean looked at him skeptically. He sized up Jamal and asked him, "How come you always like the Black heroes?"

Jamal was stunned. He wasn't ready to answer that question. He shrugged his shoulders and said, "I don't know."

Alexander commented, "Because he *is* Black, dummy."

"That doesn't mean he has to like only Black heroes," Dean argued.

Jamal protested, "I don't like only Black heroes."

"Yes, you do," Dean insisted. "Remember you brought over all of those 'Blade' movies, and my mother said they were too gory and violent for us to watch. And then we watched that 'Spawn' cartoon series from HBO over your house too. And they're all Black guys. You even made us watch the 'Boondocks' at your house on our sleepover."

Jamal felt trapped. It was all true, and he didn't know how to respond to it.

Alexander said, "So what? I liked those movies."

Sean said, "Yeah, they were cool. 'Blade' and 'Spawn' both rock!"

"Yeah, but they're always beating up on White guys," Dean said. "And that's racist."

"It's just a movie, man," Emilio spoke up.

Dean still wanted to prove his point that Jamal only chose Black heroes. He said, "Okay, so who is your favorite actor? Will Smith, right? You're always watching Will Smith movies. We've all seen 'I.Robot,' 'Wild, Wild, West,' and 'Independence Day' at least *five times* at your house."

Jamal finally spoke up for himself. "We didn't watch it that many times."

Emilio begged to differ. "We *did* watch 'I.Robot' that many times over your house."

Jamal smiled and admitted it. "That's one of my favorite movies," he said. "But I don't just like Will Smith. I like the robot, Sunny."

Sean agreed with him. "Yeah, Sunny should have like, his own movie. He'd be a robot hero in a robot world. He was awesome when he started fighting the other robots. I didn't know he could fight that good."

Emilio said, "He was their hero."

"But I'm talking about in his own movie," Sean argued.

"But you're still not getting my point," Dean said.

Alexander said, "Who cares? Jamal is Black, so of course he's gonna like Black heroes."

Jamal didn't like the sound of that either. Alexander made his choices seem too simplistic. So he argued, "I don't like every hero because he's Black. I like *Spiderman*. I like *The X-Men. Daredevil.*

Dean got excited again. He said, "Okay then, who was your favorite Jedi in the 'Star Wars' prequels? Mace Windu, right?"

Jamal started to smile again. "Mace Windu was the best," he answered.

"Yeah, Mace Windu was the best," Alexander agreed. "I always use him to fight with on the 'Star Wars' video games."

"And he's the only one with that cool purple light saber," Emilio added.

"But he wasn't the best," Dean argued. "That's why Anakin killed him."

Alexander frowned and said, "Anakin didn't kill him. He turned into a traitor and cut Mace Windu's arm off when he was about to kill the Sith Lord."

Emilio said, "Yeah, Mace Windu beat the Sith Lord all by himself until Anakin came in and stopped him. He was gonna kill the Sith Lord easily."

"Well, what about Yoda?" Dean asked them all. "He was the Jedi master. I think he was the best."

Alexander argued, "No he wasn't. Yoda couldn't even beat the Sith Lord. The Sith Lord beat Yoda, but he couldn't beat Mace Windu. He needed Anakin to help him."

"Well, what about Anakin? Anakin could beat Mace Windu," Dean told them all.

Sean shook his head and said, "No he couldn't. Anakin surprised him with a sneak attack. But he couldn't beat Mace Windu if they were really fighting, one on one."

Dean said, "Well, if Mace Windu is so strong, then how come he didn't use The Force to sense that Anakin was going to attack him, like Yoda did with the Star Troopers?"

Jamal stood there and enjoyed the argument. He didn't feel he had to say another word. Mace Windu was still the best Jedi to him, and everyone else seemed to agree but Dean.

Sean finally asked his friend, "Do you have a problem with Black heroes or something?" He wanted to know what the big deal was about.

"Yeah, so I guess you don't like Morpheus from 'The Matrix' movies, either," Alexander assumed. "He's a Black hero."

"But Morpheus is not really a superhero," Dean replied. "He was just the leader of the human revolution fighters."

Alexander said, "Duh, most leaders of revolutions are heroes. Look at the first American president, George Washington. He was the leader of the American revolution. Are you telling me that he's not a hero?"

Dean grew frustrated by the conversation. No one was getting what he was saying. "All right, just forget about it," he snapped.

"What other superheroes do you like?" Emilio asked Jamal. Dean at least had them curious about Jamal's likes and dislikes. Jamal usually kept a lot of his thoughts to himself. He did the least amount of talking in their group.

But once Emilio put him on the spot again, all eyes and ears were on Jamal.

Jamal grinned and answered, "Wolverine. He's not a Black hero."

Dean heard him and let it slide. There was no sense in continuing to try and make something out of nothing. But he was still thinking about it.

The five boys moved on and began to take turns playing each other in video games on the large television set in Dean's basement family room. They liked playing the John Madden football game. And when it was Jamal's turn to play Emilio, who beat Sean, using the Dallas Cowboys over Sean's Green Bay Packers, Jamal picked the Tennessee Titans, with the African-American quarterback Vince Young.

Jamal's choice of team for football started Dean all over again. He said, "I knew it. He always chooses Philadelphia, Atlanta and now Tennessee, just because they all have Black quarterbacks."

Sean started laughing and shook his head. "Come on, man," he commented.

Alexander said, "But they're all good players. I play with Atlanta all the time. I love using Michael Vick for quarterback. Are you kidding me? He's like the fastest guy on the field. You wait until I play with the Falcons next game."

By this time, Dean was adamant. It was his basement, his video game, and his *Marvel Universe Encyclopedia*, and he wanted to know once and for all what Jamal's problem was. So he jumped up and put the game on pause to raise his point with his African-American friend.

"Hey, what are you doing?" Emilio pouted. His Dallas Cowboys were in position to score his first touchdown or field goal.

Dean stood in front of the TV and ignored him. He looked and said, "Okay Jamal, I want to know why you even hang out with us if all you ever do is choose other Black people for everything. How come you don't choose all Black friends too?"

Alexander frowned and shook his head, tired of hearing it all. "Duh, because he lives in *Elmhurst* like we do. But I bet if he lived in Chicago with more Black people, he wouldn't even go to school or be friends with us."

Dean finally agreed with something his friends had to say. So he nodded his head to Alexander and said, "I know, that's what I mean. Jamal is a racist. And he's only friends with us because he lives out here in the suburbs. But if he lived in the city with more Black people, he probably wouldn't even talk to us."

Jamal didn't know what to say at first, but Dean was

really starting to bother him. He asked him, "Would you talk to me if I didn't live out here? I don't complain about all the *White* heroes and the actors and athletes that *you* choose. But you're always complaining about me, and who I like. So maybe *you're* the one who's racist."

That was a mouthful for Jamal. Dean had brought it all out of him. The other boys were all shocked by it themselves. Jamal was really getting upset.

But Dean continued. He said, "If I was racist, I wouldn't even invite you over my house."

Jamal snapped, "Yeah, and if I was racist, then I wouldn't invite you over to *my* house."

They had gotten so loud in their argument that Dean's mother overheard the racket from the kitchen. She decided to walk down to the basement to investigate.

She entered the room wearing a large floral apron and asked the boys, "What's going on in here?"

Dean turned to his mother and immediately spilled the beans.

"Jamal is racist, and he's only friends with us because he lives out here," he told her.

When Dean's mother looked over at Jamal for an explanation, Jamal became silent again. He couldn't believe that Dean was out to get him that badly because of his choices of African-American heroes.

Dean's mother asked him, "Is that true, Jamal?"

Jamal dropped the video game controller from his hands and felt all hot inside.

Then he began to stutter. "He, he, he's just saying that because I have different heroes from him."

"Yeah, and he's always choosing Black people. I mean, like, *always*, and in everything that we do," Dean explained to his mother.

Jamal could hardly breathe at that point. He felt like tearing Dean's blonde head off for putting him on the spot like that.

Dean's mother looked around and was confused herself.

She took a breath to compose her thoughts and emotions. She said, "Well, Dean, you can't go around dictating who your friends like. Every one of your friends are gonna have their own opinions about who they like and why."

Sean spoke up and said, "Yeah, that's what we told him."

Emilio added his two cents in and said, "But Dean just kept bringing it up, and then he put the game on pause." Emilio still wanted to win the game.

Dean got frustrated again and said, "But it's *true*, Jamal *is* a racist."

When his mother heard her son's words, she said, "Now Dean, you stop that right now. That is a very powerful word that you're using, and you don't know what it means."

"Well, you and dad use it all the time," he pouted.

Now his mother looked embarrassed. She said, "But we use it the right way. And there are still many people who make judgments based only on skin color, and that is not right."

"Well, why is it right for Jamal to make choices based on skin color?" Dean demanded to know. "He does it all the time. And that's not fair. That's just what I'm talking about."

Dean had a point, so his mother tried to gather her thoughts again.

Only now did Alexander watch and listen. He found the conversation very interesting. He wanted to see how it all would play out.

Jamal waited for Dean's mother to respond to the difficult question.

Finally, she said, "Jamal has a right to honor people from his culture, just like we have a right to honor people from ours. But that does not make him a racist. And you don't call an Italian American a racist for honoring other Italians. You don't call a Polish American a racist for honoring other citizens from Poland. And you don't call you friend, Jamal Henderson, a racist for honoring other African Americans, just like you shouldn't call Emilio Sanchez a racist for honoring other Latino Americans, or Sean Irving a racist for honoring other Jewish Americans."

Deans' mother used all of the kids' backgrounds to make her point. Alexander was so pleased with her explanation that he added his own comments.

"And you can't call me a racist for honoring Native Americans, because my great grandmother on my father's side was an Apache Indian."

Dean's mother looked at him and said, "You see that?"

Dean was still unmoved by it. "But Mom, no one else chooses *only* people from their own culture but Jamal," he complained.

"That's not true," Jamal argued. "Dean did that on purpose. He picked all the people that he knows I like already.

But I told him I like other people. He knows I like Tom Cruise, Brian Urlacher, Peyton Manning, Wolverine. I like the Red Hot Chili Peppers, Justin Timberlake, Jeff Gordon. But he kept trying to say that I only choose Black people all the time."

Dean's mother shook her head and said, "Okay, well look, you guys are all gonna have to understand that the world, and the people in the United States of America, are made up of many different cultures. But we've become all one great big melting pot. And when people in America do great things, we *all* get the credit. And none of us are going to make it as far as we can in this country by denying each other opportunities. Okay?

"Now we have an African-American senator, Barack Obama, from our own state of Illinois, who is running for president, and we *all* deserve to be proud of that. So I don't want to hear any more about this. And you all get along down here. Do you hear me, Dean?"

Dean finally calmed down and took a deep breath of his own. "Yes," he mumbled.

"Good," his mother told him. She looked at her watch and said, "Now you guys have another hour in here and then we're gonna have to call it a day."

"Aw, Mom," Dean pouted again.

"What did I say?" his mother told him. Then she glanced over at Jamal before she looked back to her son. "And Dean, you know what you need to do."

Dean dropped his head and grumbled under his breath, "Yes, ma'am."

When his mother left the basement, Jamal and Emilio went back to their video game of John Madden football in silence. The fun and camaraderie had been sucked out of the room.

After a minute of staleness, Dean waited between plays of the game to extend his right hand to Jamal's. "I'm sorry, man," he said in remorse. "My bad. And I still choose you as my friend."

Jamal smiled, feeling relieved, and took a break from the controller to accept Dean's apology with a handshake.

"Thanks," he told him. "I still choose you too."

Then Dean smiled from ear to ear. "I like Mace Windu and Morpheus too," he added. "They were cool heroes. And I like Vince Young, Allen Iverson, and Tiger Woods."

Alexander heard all of that and broke out laughing. He agreed, "There are a lot of Black heroes." Then he looked at Emilio and said, "And Spanish baseball players," with a laugh.

Emilio said, "What about Tony Romo, the quarterback for the Dallas Cowboys? He doesn't play baseball. He plays football. I'm using him now."

Alexander said, "I was just kidding you, man. I'm not a racist. And my father loves Oscar De La Hoya. He thinks he's one of the best boxers *ever*."

Jamal smiled. He thought to himself, *Oscar De La Hoya couldn't beat Floyd Mayweather Jr. though*. He had even watched their record-breaking fight with his uncle. But he didn't want to start another argument by choosing another Black hero. So he decided to keep his thoughts to himself as he usually did and continued to play his game in silence.

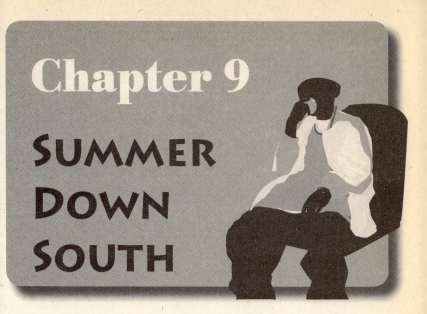

Chapter 9

SUMMER DOWN SOUTH

Chestnut stepped off the Greyhound bus in downtown Richmond, Virginia, wearing his dark blue Yankees hat and did not like what he saw. The bus station there was empty, or at least when compared to the busy crowds that he was used to up in New York. The South always seemed empty compared to Brooklyn. Chestnut loved the New York crowds, the street traffic, playgrounds, and the constant activity of the community there. But he had been sent to spend his entire summer in Richmond with his cousin, Jim-Jim. And it was so quiet down South that Chestnut swore he could hear crickets chirping all day and night.

"I don't like it down South, Mom," he pleaded to his mother back home nine hours ago. "I won't get in no trouble this summer, Mom. Please," he had begged. His mother ignored him and sent him down South to stay with her first cousin, Pam, and her husband anyway.

"Well, h-i-i-i-i, Marshall," his older cousin Pam greeted him at the bus station. Chestnut even hated how they greeted each other down South. It all seemed overdone and phony to him, as if they were actors in a movie. His friends in Brooklyn only mumbled, "What up?" to him. He would give them a cool, head nod in response and that would be it. And Chestnut liked it that way.

Anyway, his big cousin Pam bent down and kissed him on his cheek. Then she backed up and looked him over. "Boy, we're gonna have to fatten you up, I see," she told him. He looked a bit skinny for her idea of a 12-year-old. Cousin Pam figured a boy needed a little meat on his bones to protect him in their rough and tumble play.

Chestnut was hating his summer stay already. He didn't like being called by his legal name, especially not from a family member. It made it seem like she hardly knew him. But he liked the part about her fattening him up though. Good food was one thing he did like about the South. They seemed to like cooking and eating.

"Hey Chestnut," his cousin Jim-Jim walked up and greeted him. Although they were the same height and age, Jim-Jim was a meatier kid than his New York cousin. Jim-Jim was a bright tan complexion while Marshall's skin matched his nick-name. He was a perfect chestnut brown with dark brown eyes.

"I see you still wear your hat all down over your eyes," Jim-Jim commented to him.

"That's how we do it in Brooklyn, kid," Chestnut stated proudly.

Jim-Jim shook his head and smiled. They gathered Chestnut's luggage and drove across a high, curving bridge toward home on the north side of Richmond.

When they arrived at the large, two-story house, Chestnut said, "Hi" to Cousin William, who was his Cousin Pam's husband and Jim-Jim's father. Cousin William was putting a coat of dark blue touch-up paint on the outside of the house.

Chestnut grinned and nodded. "He's always working on something," he commented about Jim-Jim's dad.

Cousin William overheard him and smiled back. "A busy man leads a busy life," he said.

Chestnut walked into the house and up to the guest room, where he set his suitcase down. Jessica, Jim-Jim's nine-year-old sister, ran into the room with her best friend Kasey to greet him. They both wore ponytails and bright-colored, summer outfits.

"Hey Chestnut. My mom told me that you're staying the wh-o-o-o-ole summer with us." She made it seem like forever. Chestnut frowned at her in disgust.

He sucked his teeth and mumbled under his breath, "Yeah, unfortunately."

Jim-Jim overheard him but didn't pay it any mind. He knew Chestnut would change his mind about the South once they got busy playing in the park again. So he wasted no time getting to the fun part.

"Okay, let's go across the street to the park," he told his glum cousin.

Chestnut loved being active. He looked at his cousin and nodded. "All right."

As soon as they made it to the open park across the street from the house, Chestnut asked his cousin, "Do you still catch frogs, lady bugs, and lizards and stuff?" They were on their way toward the swings.

"Yeah, I caught a frog at the creek just yesterday," Jim-Jim answered.

Chestnut frowned up his face and said, "Yuck, man. You be buggin' out down here, Jim. You gon' have to come up to New York, boy, and get yourself schooled, and #%!*."

Jim-Jim heard his cousin's use of a bad word and shook his head. "I see you still cussin'," he commented.

"So," Chestnut responded, turning up his face.

They made it over to the swings, where several other boys were using them already.

"Yo, one of y'all gon' have to give up a swing," Chestnut announced to them.

One of the boys looked at Jim-Jim as if his cousin were crazy. "Is he your cousin from New York?" he asked.

Jim-Jim had told all of his friends that his cousin from New York was coming to stay the summer with them. The Yankees baseball hat and bold, New York accent gave Chestnut away immediately.

"Yeah," Jim-Jim confirmed. He was slightly embarrassed and nervous. Chestnut had no idea who he was dealing with out there. Just because Jim-Jim's friends were from the South didn't mean that they were pushovers.

"Oh, 'cause I was gon' have to jump that boy," a darker brown kid commented. He was shorter than Jim-Jim and

Chestnut, but with his flexing muscles pumping the swing, he looked like he could do a lot of push ups and weight lifting.

Chestnut heard his challenge and said, "What? You gon' jump over here and do what?"

All of a sudden, it got real quiet.

Jim-Jim tried to warn his cousin with a hard stare and a whisper. "Don't mess with him, man. Don't," he mumbled in a low voice.

That only made Chestnut more bold about it. "Man, I'm not scared of him. And if he say he gon' jump up and do something, then let him do it."

That was all the boy needed to hear. He jumped off the swing with a puffed up chest and stared Chestnut down. He looked at Jim-Jim with a final warning. He said, "Your cousin don't know me, man. You betta' tell him about me fast."

"Tell me what? He don't have to tell me nothing," Chestnut spit back.

The boy smiled with confidence and began to walk over toward Chestnut. The other boys jumped off of their swings and began to instigate.

"Aw, man, they 'bout to fight," they fueled.

Jim-Jim jumped in front of his cousin to stop it. "No, man. My mom told me to keep you out of trouble while you're here."

Chestnut was fired up. He said, "This ain't no trouble. This kid ain't no trouble to me. I'm just 'bout to show him how we do things Brooklyn style, son."

The other Southern boys looked around at each other and started laughing. This New York kid sure had a lot of confidence to go up against the toughest boy in their neighborhood. There were four of them there to watch and instigate.

Jim-Jim was starting to sweat. His heart was racing. Since he couldn't seem to stop or slow down his cousin's big mouth, he decided to plead to his Southern friend.

"Hey, Donald, man, my cousin gets into trouble all the time. He doesn't know what he's saying. That's why his mother sent him down here to stay with us. His mouth always gets him into trouble."

"Yeah, and his mouth 'bout to get him into trouble right now, too. I didn't even say anything to that boy."

Jim-Jim sided with Donald. He said, "Yeah, I know. You didn't say anything."

Chestnut frowned up his face in disbelief. "Yes, he did. He said he was gon' have to jump me. And don't call me no *boy* again, either," he shouted.

Donald looked around at his friends and grinned. "So, what do you want me to call you, a girl?"

His friends started laughing. Even Jim-Jim chuckled at it. He figured it was better to laugh at his cousin than to have to break up a fight.

"My name is Chestnut, son. Y'all betta learn it," the New York cousin announced to the group.

One of them heard that and started to sing the Christmas carol, "*Chestnuts roasting on an open fire . . .*"

Chestnut looked at him with daggers in his eyes and said, "What?"

The boy took in the New York kid's hardened glare and began to stutter. "I, I, I was, I was just . . ."

Chestnut cut him off and said, "Oh, I thought so."

That made the other kids laugh again. But Donald wanted to get down to business. "So you wanna fight me?" he asked Chestnut almost casually. Fighting was no big deal to Donald. He had to fight his own brothers and cousins all the time. He came from a rough, bullying family.

Chestnut tossed up his hands and said, "Yeah, let's do it." Fighting was no big deal to him either. Chestnut had to be willing to fight everyday just to play outside in his neighborhood in Brooklyn.

Jim-Jim's heart started beating fast. He had to figure out a way to stop the fight without running back across the street to his house to tell his parents. That would look wimpy. And he didn't want to leave his cousin in the middle of a fight. So he grabbed Chestnut by the arms and pulled him away.

"I said, no, man," he told him.

That finally made Chestnut angry with him. Chestnut yanked his arms away from his cousin and shouted, "Get off of me, man! If he wants to fight me, I'm gon' fight him, son."

"But he doesn't want to fight you. *You* started it," Jim-Jim said.

"No I didn't."

"Yes you did."

In the tug and pull of their shouting match, neither one of them noticed Jim-Jim's mother, his little sister Jessica, and her best friend Kasey, all running across the street and into the park to break things up.

"James, what is going on over here?" his mother called her son by his formal name.

Jim-Jim faced his mother and spilled the beans immediately.

"I'm just trying to stop Marshall from fighting but he won't listen to me."

Cousin Pam looked around at the kids and already had a good idea who the fighters would be. She asked her son just to be certain.

"Well, who is he fighting with?"

Her son faced Donald and didn't want to mention his name. But Donald spoke up so he wouldn't have to.

"We were just swinging on the swings, and then he comes over here and tells us to get off, like he owns the playground or something."

Cousin Pam looked back at Chestnut and knew that the story fit him. The Brooklyn kid was always stepping up to challenge people. It was his New York state of mind. She took a deep breath and shook her head.

"Marshall, we all use the swings at this playground. Okay? So you're just gonna have to wait your turn."

As soon as the other kids heard her speak his real name, they began to snicker.

"Marshall? His name is Marshall."

"Hey, that's Eminem's name," one of the kid's commented.

"That's Eminem's real name?" another one of the kids asked.

Donald said, "Yeah, that's that White boy. You know, Slim Shady."

"You watch what you say, Donald Bradford," Cousin Pam spoke up and told him. She pointed at him to put him on the spot. She realized that Donald was a big mouthed troublemaker in his own right, and he had often steered the other boys in the wrong direction.

Donald looked around at his friends and asked, "What did I say?"

The disregard of his loose tongue got under Pam's skin more. She looked at the boy sternly and said, "You know what . . . ?" Then she paused. She wanted to figure out the exact words to explain things to him. She took a breath and said, "You're going to find a whole lot of people who are going to judge you based on how you look, where you come from, how you act, or how you talk. And all I can do is pray for you. I pray that one day you'll understand how to get along in this world without so much . . . *hostility*. You hear me?"

She looked deep into Donald's eyes to make sure that he was paying strict attention to her. Then she looked at the rest of the boys, including Chestnut. She said, "You boys all need to learn how to let it go sometimes. Just let it *go*. Every day of your life is not about a fight."

After her speech, Pam took Chestnut and Jim-Jim by their shoulders, leading them away from the park and back across the street to the house.

Chestnut was still ticked off about the whole incident. He tried to pull away to walk across the street on his own. And as soon as they reached the sidewalk in front of the house, his big cousin let him have it.

Cousin Pam spun the boy around to face her and snatched off his Yankees baseball cap to see his full face. "You know what, Marshall, you can prepare yourself to pout all summer long if you want, but you are *not* going back home to Brooklyn until the end of August. And right now we're still only in June. So you have a *long* time to get your act together this summer, *buddy*, I'm gonna tell you that right now. You hear me? Now you get up in that house and calm yourself down for a minute."

Chestnut looked at his Cousin Pam, Jim-Jim, Jessica, and Kasey, who all seemed to be against him. Then he turned and spotted Cousin William, who had stopped painting the front of the house to stare at him as well.

Cousin Pam gave him back his hat. Chestnut marched up the cement stairs to the front door of the house and mumbled to himself, "I hate this place."

Tears swelled up into his eyes as he entered the house. He slammed the screen door behind him before he stomped upstairs to the guest room. Once he made it inside the room alone, he slumped down on the bed and began to cry openly.

"I wanna go back home to Brooklyn," he mumbled through his tears. "I hate it here. I can't stand the South."

Jessica and Kasey snuck up the stairs to listen to whatever Chestnut was doing, and they overheard him crying about Brooklyn and his disdain for the South.

"Have you ever been to Brooklyn before?" Kasey asked her friend Jessica.

"Yeah," Jessica answered. "But I don't like it like I do home. In Brooklyn, we can't even walk outside by ourselves because of all the cars and stuff. And unless they take you to the playground, you don't even have a lot of room to play outside. And even when we do go to the playgrounds, it's always crowded, and you can't even have a good time. My mother never even lets us stay out long there."

Kasey asked her, "Well, why does *he* like it in Brooklyn so much."

Jessica shrugged her shoulders. "I guess he's just used to it. But he says it's boring down here."

"Boring? No it's not," Kasey said. "We get to catch lightning bugs at night, sit out on the steps with watermelon, ride our bikes up and down the sidewalk, count the stars by moonlight—lots of stuff."

Jessica shrugged her shoulders again. "I don't know what's wrong with him. He just likes getting into trouble, that's all. I guess it's not enough trouble for him down South. Come on," she told her friend.

Outside on the front patio, Cousin Pam was having a conversation with her husband about what to do with Chestnut that summer.

Cousin William was still holding his paint brush in his hand. "You just have to keep the boy busy. I mean, as much as he says it's boring here, he doesn't know how to swim, he doesn't know how to bowl, he wears a baseball hat but he doesn't like to play baseball, and there's a lot of things he says he's never done or doesn't like to do. So we'll just have to challenge him to show us how much he can learn about real living this summer. I don't know what he even does in Brooklyn."

"Well, he likes to play basketball," Pam said.

"And we have basketball courts here. So we could organize games for him, and get all the kids involved."

Jim-Jim stood there and listened in on his parents. He spoke up and said, "But Chestnut doesn't like it when people can't play as good as he can."

Cousin William looked at his son and said, "Well, if he's that good, we'll take him around to where the bigger boys play and get him in on their game. That'll show him something."

Jim-Jim liked the sound of that. Chestnut loved a challenge. He said, "Yeah, he'll like that. Because he thinks our basketball players are all slow down South."

Cousin William started laughing. "We're all slow down South, huh? Okay, well, this summer he'll get himself a real down South education." They all started to smile, knowing that Chestnut was in for quite a few surprises.

Back inside the guest room, Chestnut wiped the tears from his face and began to stare up at the ceiling fan that spun around in circles. It cooled off his overheated body. But that was another thing he hated about the South. The heat would never allow him to relax.

Jim-Jim stood outside the doorway and knocked before he entered.

Chestnut raised his head just enough to see who it was. "What do you want?" he grumbled.

"We're about to go bowling, buy ice cream, and then go to a late movie. And we can play basketball tomorrow," his cousin answered.

Chestnut heard all of that and didn't respond. Then he asked his cousin, "To see what movie?"

"'Fantastic Four: Rise of The Silver Surfer.'"

Chestnut hadn't seen that one yet. He hadn't even seen "Spiderman III."

"Did y'all see 'Spiderman' yet?" he asked.

"Yeah, we saw that when it first came out last month."

Chestnut thought about that and wondered if they would let him see it. He also asked his cousin, "Where do y'all play basketball?"

Jim-Jim answered, "At the big courts down the street and around the corner. We have new nets and painted lines and everything now."

Chestnut finally sat up in bed. "I don't even know how to bowl," he grumbled.

Jim-Jim smiled. "Good. I can finally beat you in something then."

"You crazy, son. I just gotta learn what I'm doing first," Chestnut grumbled. Then he grabbed his hat to put it back on his head. But he still refused to budge from the bed.

Jim-Jim asked, "You're still not mad at me because of that fight are you?"

Chestnut took a breath and responded, "What fight? You wouldn't even let me fight him."

Jim-Jim took a breath of his own. "I don't want you to fight him," he said. "I know how you both are, and if you beat him up in front of all of his friends, he would want to fight you every day just like he does with his brothers and cousins. And if he beats you, you'll want to do the same thing. And that would just mess up all the fun that we can have this summer."

Chestnut stopped and listened, but he didn't particularly care about having fun with his cousin's friends that summer, nor did he feel he would lose a fight to one of them. So he told Jim-Jim so.

"That kid Donald can't beat me. And I don't want to play with any of those kids."

Jim-Jim shook his head. He just couldn't understand his cousin sometimes. He said, "You know what, man? At first, I was happy that you were coming to stay with us for the summer. But you're always complaining about something. And I get tired of that sometimes."

"So?" Chestnut shot back.

"So, this ain't New York, man," Jim-Jim snapped at him. "We do our own kind of stuff here in Richmond. And we *do* have stuff to do. So if you don't want to go to the movies, or go bowling, swimming, bike riding, and play basketball and stuff with us, then . . . " Jim-Jim stopped and looked around his room. "Then I guess you can just stay in this room and be mad all day."

"Well, whatever then, man. I don't care," Chestnut responded. He crossed his arms. He refused to let his cousin have the last word. Jim-Jim gave up and left Chestnut alone inside the room.

Chestnut mumbled to himself after his cousin left. "I didn't ask to come down here anyway. Stupid place." And he stayed right there on the bed.

Chestnut was curious when he heard all of the foot traffic heading downstairs, but he refused to budge. He would show them all just how much he hated the South by not doing anything with them. But when he heard the front door close, and everything got real quite, he began to wonder.

They didn't leave me here by myself, did they? he thought. *I'm gonna tell my mom if they did.* He hopped up off the bed and finally went to investigate downstairs.

Chestnut rushed out of the guest room and scrambled down the stairs yelling, "Hello! Hello!"

"Yeah, what's wrong, Marshall?" Cousin William answered from the living room. He was watching a golf tournament on TV. His feet were propped up on the coffee table.

Chestnut looked at him and froze. He asked, "Where did everybody else go?" He was hoping and praying they didn't leave him there.

"They all went to the movies to see the Silver Surfer in 'Fantastic Four,'" Cousin William answered.

Chestnut heard that and his heart dropped. He wanted to go to the movies, too. He stood there heartbroken, but not wanting to admit it.

He asked, "Are they coming back after that?"

William shook his head. "No, they said they're going bowling after that."

"But what about to eat?" Chestnut wanted to know. "They're not coming back home to eat?"

Cousin William told him, "No, they'll get something to eat while they're out."

Chestnut felt like a fool. He would miss out on everything. "But what about me?" he whined. "I'm hungry." He felt so bad about being left behind that he was ready to break down again. How could they leave him like that?

Cousin William said, "Oh, if you're hungry, I can fix you some leftovers from last night." Then he stood up from his lounge chair.

Chestnut mumbled, "Leftovers?" That didn't sound good to him at all.

"Yeah, chicken dumplings, with home made gravy and

rice. And I can heat up some new biscuits for you if you like."

His big cousin started walking toward the kitchen, but Chestnut had lost his appetite and fresh tears were welling up in his eyes.

Chestnut made a slow walk into the kitchen behind his big Cousin William, but he was steady fixing his plate and not paying Chestnut much mind. Cousin William was even whistling.

"By the way, take that hat off inside the house, Marshall," he demanded. "Then I need you to go inside the bathroom and wash your hands."

It was just too miserable for a 12-year-old. So, with uncontrollable tears of anger rolling down his face, Chestnut washed his hands in the bathroom, using a bottle of Soft Soap sitting on the sink.

"I hate it here," he mumbled to himself again. But before he walked out of the bathroom, Chestnut wiped the tears from his eyes on the same paper towels he used to dry his hands. He couldn't let his big cousin see a Brooklyn kid cry.

Cousin William had a plate full of food waiting at the kitchen table. It was nice and hot. A cold glass of lemonade sat beside the plate.

"*Bon apetit*," Cousin William said, using the French phrase for "enjoy your meal."

As soon as Chestnut sat down to eat, sad-eyed and with no appetite, Cousin William added, "And a word to the wise, Marshall. I understand that you may have a little bit of a problem staying here this summer with us, but from what

I understand, it's already a done deal. You're not going back home until the end of summer. But we're not here to punish you—we want you to have a good time with us. However, if you want to punish yourself by not taking advantage of the good fortune you have of being around people who love and care about you down here in the South, then be my guest."

"But let me warn you," he continued. "Tonight is just the first night of more than sixty that you'll be here with us. If I were you, I would do the math and add up the fact that I would rather have a good time for sixty something days, than to spend all of my time *pouting* and feeling like you do right now."

After that, Cousin William went back to watching the golf tournament on TV, leaving Chestnut alone to eat and figure out for himself how he would spend the rest of his summer with them in Richmond.

Chestnut stared at his plate of food and thought to himself, *I could have been at the movies right now, or going bowling and getting pizza or something. And I'm sitting here stuck with leftovers.*

Then he dropped his fork on the table in frustration. He knew that Cousin William was right. If he continued to pout and not enjoy himself, he would be in for a lonnng, miserable summer.

Chestnut mumbled himself. "I might as well do what they do." Then very slowly he picked up his fork to finish eating.

Chapter 10

I Ain't No Sissy

"**W**atch me jump off this tree and land on my feet like Spiderman," T.C. told his friends from where he stood on top of a tree limb. The thick branch stretched out wide and turned upward at its end like a giant brown arm in a body building contest.

T.C.'s friends looked up at him from the ground as if he were crazy. The tree limb that he stood on was at least ten feet above the ground, like the top of a basketball hoop backboard. Few of his friends were even willing to climb that high, let alone jump down from that height.

"You're crazy, T.C. You're gonna break your legs up there that high," one of his friends yelled at him.

It was a bright and sunny afternoon at the recreational park on the west side of St. Louis, Missouri, and 11-year-old

T.C., his three sisters, and his friends enjoyed themselves in afternoon play.

"Aw, man, I can do it. Watch me," T.C. insisted.

Right as he got ready to jump, his younger sister Sharon stopped him.

"Uuuwwww, I'm gon' tell mom if you do that. You gon' hurt yourself again and have to go back to the hospital," she told him.

It seemed that for some odd reason her brother was constantly challenging himself to be a dare devil.

T.C. sucked his teeth at her and hollered, "Shut up, girl! You better not tell on me!"

Sharon said, "If you break your leg, I won't have to tell. Mom'll find out anyway at the hospital," and she strutted away to rejoin her older sisters, who jumped rope near the basketball courts.

"You better listen to your sister, man," another one of T.C.'s friends warned him. T.C., however, remained determined to prove his bravery.

"Aw, I don't care about her. I ain't no sissy," he responded. "I'm not afraid of anything. If Spiderman can do it, so can I."

Before anyone could get another word out, T.C. launched himself from the tree limb with his knees up and arms up high, like Spiderman jumping over a building. Then, he actually landed on his feet with a hard thump before he rolled forward like a professional gymnast.

Seeing that he had made the jump without seriously injuring himself, T.C.'s friends were amazed.

"Aw, man, that was tight. How did you do that?"

"Yeah!" they all shouted.

T.C. climbed back to his feet and grinned. He told them, "Like I said, I'll do anything."

"Anything?" some of his friends began to question aloud. They were starting to form their own crazy, dare devil ideas for T.C. to try. But before they could challenge him, T.C.'s two older sisters came running to the rescue.

"TRAY-CEE! What did mom tell you about that, boy? I am so tired of you trying to hurt yourself all the time!" his oldest sister, Paula, yelled at him. She, Sharon, and Adrienne, the second oldest, were all over him.

"I told him not to," Sharon spoke up again.

"And I told *you* not to tell on me," T.C. yelled back at her.

"She *didn't* tell on you," Paula said. "I saw you jump out that tree with my own eyes."

"Yeah," Adrienne added with her two cents.

T.C. was stuck and embarrassed. He hated that he had to listen to two older sisters and an instigating younger one. Boy, did he wish he had two older brothers instead. Older brothers would understand him more. Maybe his father would understand him more too, if he were around. His mother just didn't get it; boys will be boys. And boys liked to dare each other. Or at least T.C. did.

"Well, you can tell mom all you want to," he boasted. "I'm gonna do it anyway. I don't care."

"All right, we'll see about that," Paula told him.

"We *will* see," T.C. snapped. He refused to back down from her. No girl told him what to do. So what if she was his older sister? She was a *girl*. And girls couldn't hang with boys. They were all too fragile. Or least that's what T.C. thought. So when his three sisters marched off toward home, he remained defiant.

"What are you gonna do now?" one of his friends asked him.

T.C. shrugged his shoulders. "Go back to playing," he answered. Even though the bottom of his feet were burning from the impact of his jump, T.C. ignored the pain and went back to his reckless play.

A half an hour later, one of T.C.'s friends spotted his mother and three sisters marching toward them in unison through the park.

"Uh-oh, T., here comes your mom and sisters, man."

T.C. looked in their direction with his large, wide eyes full of terror. His heart began to race inside of his chest like thunder, while his friends wondered what he would do next. They all felt it was curtain time for him. The tough guy act would disappear, and their courageous friend would go back to being an embarrassed little kid who had to listen to his mother like the rest of them.

T.C. looked into his friends' faces, and he could see the doom they all predicted for him. Their eyes were just as wide as his were. But then T.C. took a deep breath and calmed his nerves.

I'm not gonna be scared of her anymore, he told himself. *I'm not!*

He boldly stood up straight and thought of what his next move would be before his mother and sisters could reach him.

Either I take it like a man and argue for my side, or I run away from her, he told himself. *Man, I wish I had a dad. Then I wouldn't have to go through this. A dad would understand that boys like to climb trees and skateboard and play fight. We're just doing boy stuff, and sometimes you get hurt with it. That's all.*

T.C. began to think about it so much that he forgot how close his mother and sisters were. They continued to approach him. He could even hear them talking.

"There he is, Mom," he overheard Adrienne pointing him out to their mother.

T.C. stood in silence and watched his mother's raving eyes and swinging arms as she approached him. She wore stylish, designer blue jeans, a yellow tank top, gold jewelry, and shiny gold heels that all stood out in the sunlight. Her colorful outfit seemed to be the only thing he paid attention to. It was like he was in a dream. He was momentarily hypnotized by what would happen to him next, just like his friends wondered. So they all stood there, watching and waiting.

When T.C.'s mother reached him, she immediately tried to grab his left arm. "Boy, what did I tell you about acting a fool out in these streets? Didn't I tell you about that?"

Just as his mother reached for him, T.C. sidestepped her and moved out of the way. That caused his mother to stumble forward, awkwardly.

"Boy, come here!" she yelled at him.

"Why?" T.C. asked her. "What I do?"

He wanted his mother to explain the reason for her anger. Why couldn't he be a rough and tumble boy? And why did she have to name him Tracy anyway, forcing him to use the initials T.C.? Didn't she know that Tracy was a *girl's* name? So T.C. felt that he was doomed from birth to *prove* that he was *not* girly.

His mother answered. "Tracy, I already told you, I am *tired* of paying hospital bills for stitches and operations and broken bones with you. Now why can't you just play that PlayStation game I bought for you?"

"I don't like playing that game all the time," T.C. told her. "I like being outside with my friends."

"Well, if your friends know how to *act*, then they're all welcome to come over to the house and play your game with you."

T.C. looked at his sisters and said, "Yeah, but then Adrienne and Sharon are always getting in our way. That's why we'd rather be outside instead of arguing with them."

"You don't own our house," Adrienne snapped at him, standing beside her mother.

T.C. looked at his mother and said, "See?"

"Well, what does she have to do with you jumping out of trees and carrying on, Tracy?" his mother asked him. "How are you gonna blame your sisters for that, since you like to blame them for everything?"

"I blame them for telling you, too," he mumbled.

His smart mouth and defiant attitude made his mother want to grab him again. She reached out at him a second time and said, "Boy, if you don't get over here . . ."

Again, T.C. was too quick for her, causing his mother to stumble around in broad daylight at the St. Louis park, trying to grab him. Even his friends began to smile and giggle at her awkwardness.

Seeing that their mother was having problems getting

a hold of her younger brother, Paula, the oldest, decided to grab him herself. She used more speed, foot movement and outstretched arms to make sure that T.C. didn't sidestep her as well. But when she succeeded in grabbing him, it only irritated T.C. and made him angrier.

"Get off of me, girl!" he shouted and yanked away from his sister.

That made his mother take off running after him in her shiny golden heels. She was determined to beat him silly when she caught him.

T.C. saw that and broke into a full sprint, putting football moves on his mother to avoid her. That made his friends laugh out loud. Then his mother then became livid.

She pointed at him and promised, "Tracy, when I catch you, I'm gonna tear a brand new fire to your behind." Then she eyed his laughing-out-loud friends. "And I know every one of your mothers too. So don't think for a *minute* that I'm not gonna tell them about this. Because I am."

None of the boys liked the sound of that. T.C.'s crazy antics were getting them all into trouble.

"I didn't laugh," one of the boys commented.

T.C. eyed him as if he were a traitor. *Why did he have say anything? Sissy,* he thought to himself.

"I didn't laugh either," another one of his friends stated.

Sissy number two, T.C. thought. But his other three friends did laugh, and they were now nervous about it.

"I didn't mean to laugh," another one spoke up.

Sissy number three, T.C. thought. He continued to eye his friends from a distance to avoid his mother's reach.

His mother said, "Well, I'm gonna speak to all of your mothers anyway."

The boys didn't know if they should be mad at her or at their friend. They were all hurt, nervous, and confused by it all.

Meanwhile, T.C. refused to give in. Finally his mother gave up trying to catch him.

"Well, you can stay out with your uncle tonight, Tracy, because you're *not* coming back home with me, she said. "I can tell you that right now. And you *may* be staying over there with him for *good*."

T.C. didn't like the sound of that. His Uncle Haley kept a messy and noisy house. It was extra hot there with no central air unit and three small fans that rarely got the job done. Uncle Haley's apartment also had the creepy, crawling house insects called roaches, and T.C. definitely didn't like that. The dark brown roaches grossed him out and made him feel fidgety. So he had a new dilemma on his hands as his mother and sisters turned and stormed away.

His friends looked at him for another response. "What are you gonna do now? Your mom's not gonna let you back in the house?" they asked him.

T.C. was still upset by most of his friends wimping out on him in front of his mother, but he took another deep breath and answered their question anyway.

"I'm just gonna have to stay with my uncle for awhile then."

His Uncle Haley lived in the apartment complex on the

opposite side of the park from where T.C. lived with his mother and sisters.

———

When T.C. left his friends and walked through the park toward his uncle's apartment, his Uncle Haley met him at the edge of the playground.

"What's this I'm hearing about you fighting with your mother out at the park today?" he asked his nephew.

Uncle Haley had a big, round belly and lots of facial hair, making him look like a human grizzly bear in a light blue jeans jumper. He didn't look too pleased that day either.

T.C. looked at the cell phone on his uncle's hip and realized that his mother had told him her side of the story already.

"She don't understand that I'm a boy, Uncle Haley," he said. "And she's always complaining about the things we do."

"What, you mean like riding your skateboard out in the middle of the street, and getting hit by that car? And how about the time when you tried to jump a ramp on your dirt bike and broke your arm? Better yet, what about the time you and your friends decided to have a rock fight and you ended up nearly getting your eye put out before the doctor closed up your face with seven stitches?"

T.C. grinned and said, "That was all boy stuff."

"No, it's not. It's all *stupid* stuff," his uncle told him. "I didn't do all of that craziness when I was a boy."

"You didn't have the name *Tracy* either," his nephew mumbled.

Uncle Haley looked him over and got the point. He nodded to himself and said, "Oh, so that's what this is all about? You think your name makes you less of a boy? Is that why you feel you need to do all of this crazy stuff you do?"

T.C. stood there and didn't answer. Then he said, "I tell them all the time not to call me that. But that's my real name, so what can I do? But when I'm old enough, I'm gonna change it.

"My mom wanted all girls anyway," he assumed. "That's why she named me that. She never even wanted a boy. She don't even like buying me clothes and stuff."

T.C. really believed his thoughts. So he sunk his head low and felt depressed.

His uncle told him, "That's ridiculous. Your mother loves you. And you're not the only man named Tracy. There was even a cartoon series called Dick Tracy, that they did a movie on."

"Yeah, but that was his *last* name," T.C. argued.

His uncle was at a loss for words for a minute. He finally said, "Well, acting out against your mother and getting yourself hurt all the time is not gonna change that. Why don't you just tell her to call you by your middle name or something?"

"I do. I always tell people to call me T.C. for Tracy Calvin. But my mom and my sisters always call me Tracy anyway."

Uncle Haley frowned and said, "That's not true. I've heard them all call you T.C. before."

"Yeah, but then they call me *Tracy* again whenever they get mad at me about something."

"Well, stop making them all mad then," his uncle

advised him. But as soon as the words left his mouth, he realized how hard that would be. Kids would be kids, and the frying pan of youth would heat up and cool off almost daily with them. A parent would need to raise four angels to expect no heated arguments or skirmishes between them. Uncle Haley couldn't see that happening any time soon with Paula, Adrienne, Tracy, and Sharon. He laughed it off and said, "Well, maybe that's a bit much to ask. But now that I see how you feel about things, I'll talk to your mother about it."

"Right now?" T.C. asked him. He still didn't want to go over to his uncle's house. He hoped they could straighten everything out with his mother immediately so he could return home to his air-conditioned room and play his video games. Since he was the lone boy in a house with only three bedrooms, T.C. was allowed to sleep in the large family room on a pull-out sofa. His mother and older sister, Paula, had their own rooms, and Adrienne and Sharon had to share a room.

But Uncle Haley shook off the idea of T.C. returning home anytime soon. He said, "Your mother doesn't want to hear anything about that right now. I'll have to call her back later on, once she calms herself down. You know how your mother can get."

T.C. did know. His mother was a serious yeller. So he sighed and began to think about his uncle's hot, messy, roach-infested apartment.

"So, what are you gonna do next time to make sure I don't have to keep putting you out of the house?"

T.C.'s mother asked him over his uncle's cell phone that evening.

T.C. was already feeling hot and sticky at his uncle's tiny apartment. Then he watched his Uncle Haley smash a big brown roach against the kitchen counter top before he grimaced and responded to his mother.

"I'll be good, Mom. I promise."

"I don't believe you," she told him. "You *like* doing crazy stunts. Maybe I need to get you involved in football or something. You know they have tryouts this week. And since you love running and jumping and smashing into things so much, you might as well do it with some pads on."

T.C. cheered up instantly. He loved the sound of that idea. His mother had never talked about him playing youth football before. She must have talked to his uncle about it earlier.

He said, "Yeah, I can try out I . . .

His mother cut him off, "But if you continue to be hardheaded about all this extra stuff you feel you need to get into, then I'll take you off the team and send you over to your uncle's on a regular basis. Because I'm tired of it."

"Okay," T.C. muttered. "So can I come back home now?" he asked his mother.

It was not quite 10 P.M. yet. His Uncle Haley could drive him back home in less than five minutes. That's how close he lived. But his mother denied him.

"No, I think you need to stay over there for the night and he can bring you back home before he goes to work in the morning," she answered.

T.C. whined, "Aw, Mom, but . . ."

"What did I say?" she snapped at him.

"Okay," he whimpered

When T.C. hung up the phone with his mother, he noticed that his Uncle Haley was smiling at him. But T.C. wasn't smiling. He knew he would worry all night long about creepy roaches crawling on him while he slept. They never did, but he couldn't help from thinking that they might.

Uncle Haley said, "Now, I've talked your mother into letting you play football this year, and I told her to make sure she calls you T.C. instead of Tracy. But you have to do the rest, you hear me? That means getting along with your sisters, and not getting yourself hurt anymore out in the streets. You save your daredevil moves for the football field now."

T.C. nodded and felt grateful, but he still didn't want to spend the night on his uncle's rusty sofa. So he figured he had to get along with his mother and sisters by any means necessary to save himself from having to spend any more nights at his uncle's apartment.

"All right," he grumbled.

When his uncle went to bed that night, T.C. continued to respond to every little noise he heard in the apartment, hoping and praying that none of the roaches would crawl on him and gross him out.

I ain't no sissy, he told himself as he tried to sleep, *I just hate roaches.*

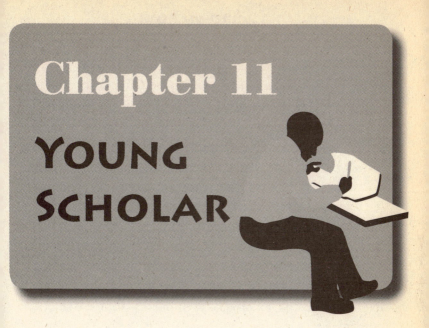

Chapter 11

YOUNG SCHOLAR

Hi, my name is William Davidson Jr., and I live in Santa Monica, California, right next to Beverly Hills, Hollywood, and Los Angeles. I love living here, I really do. Almost everyday I get to meet rich and famous actors, musicians, athletes, and their lawyers, managers, accountants, stylists, personal assistants, trainers, psychologists and even their live-in chefs! I get to visit their mansions, play with their kids, ride in their expensive cars, fly in private jet air planes, take cruises on private yachts, and everything. But my parents, who are both entertainment lawyers and know almost everyone, have always kept me humble by reminding me how hard they had to work to reach where they are today. Even though my parents drive nice cars and we live in a very nice house and neighborhood,

I've learned how to make good decisions by thinking about everything around me to prepare for my future.

A big part of my goals in life is to excel in school at the Santa Monica Academy. We call it SMA for short, and it's a really good school. I've been getting straight A's there since kindergarten, and I really love it. We have every science, art, music, and athletic program that you can think of. We also have separate buildings and playing fields for each subject and sport, like a mini college for kids.

My school is awesome! We have our own school news-paper, a television station, and our sports teams have three private buses with our Panther spirit logo painted on them in gold and black, all bought with the donations of the rich parents whose kids have attended school there. I'll probably donate money to the school when I'm grown and sending my kids to SMA too, that is if I still live in Santa Monica. My parents told me to always leave my options open to explore everything, even to live in Africa, Australian, or Japan if I want to. That would be exciting!

I'm one of the few African-American kids at my school, but I don't mind it at all. My parents have shown me how to make an impact in school, even without playing sports, like a lot of the other African-American boys do who attend school at SMA. I have admit that I wanted to play sports too, but it was just too competitive. We have some really great athletes at our school who are sons and daughters of professional athletes. So, to stay involved in sports, I decided to take stats at the football, basketball, and baseball games. Now I record what players have the most touchdowns, rushing yards, passing yards, receiving yards, tackles, sacks and interceptions in football. In basketball, I record what players have the most points, rebounds, assists and steals. And in baseball I record what players have the most home runs, the highest batting averages, runs batted in, pitching records, and outs on defense.

I basically keep track of what everyone reads on the back of professional playing cards and in the sports pages of the newspapers. Once the guys on the teams at my school found out what I was doing, they all wanted to stay in touch with me to get their stats during the season. So I became one of the most popular kids in school with the athletes. And even though some of them would still tease me for being an extra smart kid, they all started to love seeing and talking to me. Or at least when they're having good games. But when they were not having good games, they were not so open to talk to me. I guess everyone likes good news more than bad news.

Anyway, the popularity that I gained with athletes by taking game stats made me think about how I could get involved with the students who were more into art, math, science and music. I didn't want to give all of my attention to athletes and leave the regular students out. So for the art students, I talked to the editors at the school newspapers about publishing the best artwork and interviewing the artists. For the math students, the editors and I kept statistics on a school-wide math bee, just like we did with the school spelling bee and debate team, where I'm also a junior member. For the science students, we spotlighted all science project winners with interviews and posted a schedule of all upcoming science events at school, just like we did with the sports schedule. And for the music students, I decided to organize school band trials just for fun, to see who could come up with their own hot groups for school performances and concerts. The musicians at the school came up with their own band names, poster designs, and everything. It was great!

When the teachers found out everything I was involved in as a sixth grader at school, they started asking me how I came up with my ideas and where I found the time to do it all.

Well, since I'm an only child, I have no one to play with at home. And there's no one for my parents to give their attention to but me. So I'm able to use my parents to the max. And they love helping me out with everything. They say that they will always make sure they spend time working with me on whatever I have in mind.

I learn a lot from my parents. While they work on contracts for their clients, I work on school ideas for my classmates. But most of my parents' ideas require them to beg corporate sponsors and private investors for financial backing. Many of the rich parents at my school are eager to give almost any amount to help keep their kids excited about their education. The only thing the school told me was that I could not make any personal profit from any of my ideas. They were concerned that I could easily turn our school into a bad example of irresponsible capitalism, especially with so many wealthy parents who could afford to write big checks for the benefits and desires of their children. But that was okay by me. I didn't do anything for the money anyway. It was all for fun.

My parents explained that the experience I was gaining at SMA would follow me as a part of my academic and extracurricular resume wherever I decided to go to for high school and college. They told me that if I continued with my strong innovations and work habits, I would make my life as a adult twenty times easier.

"Life is filled with rewards for people who boldly use their gifts and talents to build on their ideas," my parents told me. "That's why we've always gone out of our way to surround you with the best positive influences. We want you to stay inspired and know that you can do anything you put your mind to and become anything you would like to be."

The next thing I knew, I had a bunch of kids at my school who all wanted to work with me on every new idea I came up with. Even their parents wanted to talk to me about my ideas. But I remembered not to get a big head from all of the attention that I was getting. So instead of getting paid for anything, I told my parents to ask our school officials if I could raise money for charity to give to the students at less fortunate schools in Los Angeles, Carson, and Compton. I had always read about how bad things were in less wealthy school districts, and I wanted to do something to help them.

"Wow! You're really raising your boy right!" our principal, Dr. Paul Collinsworth, told my parents. He said he was very proud to have me as a student at Santa Monica Academy, and I was given the school's first ever Great Young Citizen Award for academic excellence, ingenuity and community service. I even helped to create a scholarship fund for kids who could not afford to attend school at SMA.

All this activity led to me being on the local Los Angeles news and in the *Los Angeles Times* newspaper with the same movie stars, athletes, and musicians my parents worked with. My parents were really excited about that. I was invited to attend a Young American Leadership Council program in Washington, DC, to meet the president and about two hundred other kids from all over the country. We would get to visit historical and government buildings for an entire week during the school year.

Wow! That was really special. But I still didn't let it go to my head. I was just a kid having fun and loving to learn.

"So, how does it feel to be The Superkid?" my best friend Walter Pearson asked me at school one day.

I just smiled and didn't think much about it at first. I wasn't trying to be any special kid per se, I was just being me. I liked being useful. But I guess I got my desire to be of service from my parents. All I've ever seen them do is use their brains and hard work to help people, so I was just following in their footsteps.

After all of the attention I received from everyone—the school, the county, the television networks, the local newspapers and the National Leadership Council—Walter's insistence on calling me "The Superkid" began to catch on at school.

"Hey, Superkid," the other students began to greet to me in the hallways.

After about a week of that, I didn't like it. It seemed as if they were all mocking me to make fun of my recent achievements. So I asked Walter to stop calling me that.

"Why? You are The Superkid, aren't you?" he asked. "Don't you have a flying cape in your locker with straight A's down the side? Can't you jump a tall building with a single thought, and stop bullets with a flash of your sharpened pencil?"

He had a whole audience of kids laughing at me. Walter had always been competitive with me, but he had never tried to purposefully hurt my feelings like that before. That's when I knew that he was becoming jealous of me, and he was influencing the other kids to feel the same way. But what could I do about it? He was my best friend.

At dinner that night my parents immediately knew that something was bothering me. I didn't have my normal spontaneous energy.

My mother looked at me and asked, "Is something wrong?"

I was rarely a kid to have a sour mood about anything. Like I said, I loved everything about my life. But now I had a reason to feel bad, and I didn't want to talk about it.

"No," I answered.

My mother knew me better than that, but she never tried to pressure me before I was ready to talk. So she stared at me like a mother would and said, "William, whenever you're ready to talk to us about what's on your mind, you know that we're here for you. Okay?" And that was all that she said to me.

After another ten minutes of me coming up with no solution to my problem, I sat down with my parents in our study like I always did.

My mother and father were both waiting for me there. They tried to act as if they hadn't been preparing themselves to talk to me, but I knew my parents better than that. They were always ready to think up a solution to people's problems. It was their job. They were both lawyers. So I pleaded my case.

"Because of all the things that I've done recently, and all the like . . . *attention* I've been getting because of it, my friend Walter started calling me 'The Superkid' at school, and now he has everyone else saying it. And I can tell that he's jealous of me now and making fun of me and everything. And I *know* I shouldn't let it bother me, but it *does*."

I tried to hold myself together and just tell the story as is, but I got all choked up inside and tears ran out of my eyes. I just felt hurt and confused. Why was it such a bad thing to be smart? No one ever made fun of the athletic guys for scoring touchdowns, or making the last shot in a basketball game, or a home run in baseball. So why was my best friend making fun of me for winning awards for my ideas?

My father looked me in the eyes and shook his head before he commented. He even had to take off his reading glasses. That's when I knew how bothered he was. My mother just looked at him and sighed. She had nothing to say, and that was very unusual.

So I stood there thinking that maybe my parents weren't ready for my discussion. What was so complicated about being a smart kid?

My father finally answered. "William, there's just no escape in this world for a person's need for equilibrium."

I looked at my father and was still confused. I didn't want to stand there and try and figure out what he had just said. I just wanted to understand my feelings.

"I don't understand. Are you saying that Walter's doing that to feel equal to me?" I asked.

My father nodded his head and said, "Yes, he is. He's hoping that you'll back down and not be so smart next time. So if he hurts your feelings this way, he believes that you'll avoid this hurt next time by shying away from being who you are. And once you're no longer the so-called 'Superkid' who gets better grades and comes up with more ideas than Walter, then he can feel equal to you and continue to be your best friend."

That didn't make any sense to me. "But I've never made fun of him whenever he beat me in anything," I said. "And I've always tried to help him to improve his grades."

Before my father could respond to me, my mother said, "Well, let me ask you a question about Walter, William. Why do you think it is that you chose him to be your best friend?"

I was shocked. I don't know if I've ever thought about that before.

"I don't know," I answered. "I guess we've had a lot of the same interests, and we've been around each other a lot."

"So your friendship is only about familiarity?" my mother asked me.

I was still confused. Does anybody know how or why they chose their best friends?

I said, "I don't know, I just . . . I just don't like him calling me that."

My father took a deep breath and rubbed his hand over his face. "William," he began, "there's just no easy way for your mother and me to say this, but there comes a time in life when your best friends become your *old* friends, and your *new* friends become your best friends. And none us may like it when that happens, but when your interests change, and you find yourself moving forward into new directions, you'll have some old friends who will not make that move with you, and some new friends who will."

"In fact, you'll find some old friends who will actually try to stop you from moving forward," my father said. "And what are you going to do about that? You plan on throwing all of your ideas away to keep a friend?"

It was a hard question for me to answer. I loved my ideas. My ideas helped me to connect with people. They made me feel like I was a part of a larger community. And no friend would ever stop me from thinking about new things. *Ever*! So I shook my head and answered, "No." My ideas were too important to me.

That's when my mother walked over from her chair and hugged me. She said, "William, baby, I hate that you have to go through this, but we all have to at some point or another. I had to pull away from my own family. None of them believed that I could even be a lawyer. But your father did. And that's when he became *my* best friend," she chuckled.

My father smiled back at her. "And your mother became my best friend when I realized that she understood my goals, and all of the time it took for me to prepare for the bar exam."

"And not only that, but your mother was *fine*," he added with a wink.

"*Was* fine?" my mother asked him.

My father corrected himself and said, "*Is* fine."

I was smiling after that. My parents were always fun. And they always told me the truth. So I trusted them.

"Baby, you're gonna meet new friends all the time," my mom explained. "And I know that this is painful for you right now, but I'd rather have you experience this pain and get through it early, so you'll know exactly what you'll be up against in high school, in college, *and* in your professional life. So when I asked you that question about how you chose your best friend, well, now you're gonna have to learn *how* to. And just because we all have a *first* friend, who is usually a person we grew up around, he or she may not be our *last* friend. But before we jump to conclusions, maybe Walter Pearson doesn't know how much his taunts bother you."

I didn't comment on that. It seemed to me Walter knew. I had told him several times to stop calling me 'The Superkid', but that only made him say it more.

My father said, "Well, when you go back to school tomorrow, you just tell him what you told us. 'Why is being smart and helpful a bad thing?' And you see what he says then. But if being called 'The Superkid' is the worse thing they have to call you, well, I can live with that. Because you *are* super. You're a super inspiration to those kids you helped out in South Central Los Angeles, in Carson, in Compton, and to all the new kids who will receive scholarship money to attend school at Santa Monica."

"And do you feel bad about any of that?" my mother asked.

"No," I answered. "Of course not."

"Good," my father said. "So you let Walter know again tomorrow that you don't appreciate his new nickname, but that you'll just have to live with it, because you will *not* stop being William Davidson, Jr. And if he has a problem with the things that your mind tells you to do, then that's *his* problem, not yours."

When I went to bed that night, I was feeling good about myself again, and more determined. As a matter of fact, once I thought about it, I hadn't had that much in common with Walter for a few years already. I just continued to call him my best friend because I always did. But that didn't mean I had to continue feeling that way. So I prepared myself to say what was on my mind to him that next morning.

Well, when I arrived at school that morning, Walter was already waiting for me. He was standing inside the front yard with his mother at his side. I didn't know what was going on, but Walter didn't look too happy about it, nor did his mother. As soon as I approached them, his mother pushed him forward.

"Go ahead, Walter. What do you have to say?" Walter looked me in my eyes for a second before he looked down at my shoes. "You look at William when you tell him!" his mother ordered him.

Walter looked back up at me and took a deep breath. He said, "I apologize."

Before I could respond to him, his mother said, "You apologize for what?"

"I apologize for making fun of you," he said to me.

I remembered that Walter's parents were always forcing him to do the right thing. But he would only apologize when someone made him. A lot of times, he didn't really mean it. And he didn't look sorry to me at all. He looked like he was angry and embarrassed.

I later found out that Walter had been caught writing bad jokes about me in the bathroom stalls and had been forced to clean it up after school. He also was put on disciplinary probation by Dr. Collinsworth.

I didn't know if our friendship could ever be healed after that. But I was no longer sad about it, nor did I hold it against Walter.

I decided that my parents were right, it was time for me to choose friends with similar interests, and not just kids from my own environment. I had to become closer friends with kids who felt the way I did about using their brain power to make things better and for service around the country and the world. So I went to Washington, DC, met the president, and had a ball with all of the other young leaders of America. And now I have a whole e-mail list of new friends. And together, we brainstorm new ideas and make positive choices for the future, just like my parents had taught me to do.

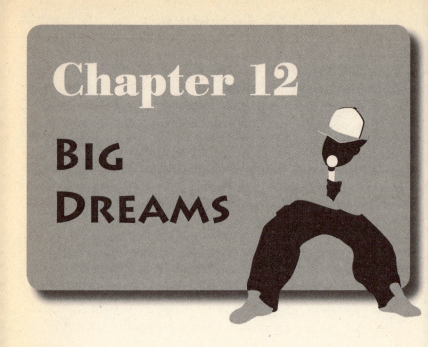

Chapter 12

BIG DREAMS

Taylor watched the Autobots' leader, Optimus Prime, on the big screen and listened to his last words of narration at the end of the "Transformers" movie. Taylor was pumped, loving everything he just saw.

"Wow, that movie was *it*!" he told his five baseball teammates, who had all watched the movie that afternoon with him.

"Yeah, you see how Optimus Prime cut off Bonecrusher's head with that giant blade?" one of his teammates commented.

"You see Megatron pull Jazz's limbs apart?" asked another.

"Remember that part when Bumble Bee changed his car into a brand new Camaro? That was crazy," said another.

They were all leaving the movie theater in Southfield, Michigan, right outside of Detroit, on the 4th of July. Their neighborhood baseball coach, William Jackson, had taken the six Red Sox teammates to the movies in his Ford Expedition truck as an extra treat for making the city-wide finals in the 11- and 12-year-old age group. The team lost in the semi-final game in a heartbreaking, 11-9 nail biter, but in no way would that loss ruin their summer vacation. These boys had a whole life of future accomplishments ahead of them, and they had played a heck of a season, with a 12-2 record.

When the boys made it to Coach Bill's black Expedition, Taylor suggested, "Hey Coach, what if your truck is really a Transformer, and it transforms while we're still inside of it? Would we all fall out, or would we still be hanging on his arms and legs?"

Coach Bill grinned at the idea as he opened the doors with his automatic key. But before he could respond, Damion, the star pitcher of the team, spoke up.

"All right, Taylor, the movie's over with, man. You can cut off your wild imagination now," he said. Damion had listened to enough of Taylor's creative ramblings for one day. He didn't want to hear it anymore. Showtime was over.

"Now, we're going back to where we live," Damion said. "Ain't no Transformers in Detroit. No Pirates. No Princes. No talking animals. None of that crazy stuff."

"We do have Tigers, Pistons, Lions and Red Wings in Detroit though," Coach Bill commented with a chuckle. He was naming the city's baseball, basketball, football and hockey teams. He said, "But a lively imagination is good for you. And I want you guys to be able to dream about being anything you want. That's why I spend so much time with you guys outside of baseball. Maybe Taylor will make his own movies one day," the coach commented.

That made Taylor real excited. He had thought about making movies, but he hadn't said it out loud to anyone yet. He didn't want anyone, like Damion, to tease him about it. But after Coach Bill said it first, Taylor pulled together enough courage to agree. "Yeah, that would be cool," he commented.

Damion frowned at the idea immediately. He asked, "You know how much money it takes to make movies? Nobody has that kind of money around here."

They all climbed into the Expedition and buckled their seat belts. Coach Bill pulled off into traffic and headed back to the west side of Detroit. "We have plenty of people in Detroit who have enough money to make movies. You just have to get to know those people."

"Well, that don't mean they're gonna give him any money," Damion argued.

"Okay, Damion, a few more years from now, let's say you become the best high school pitcher in Detroit. Do you realize that the Detroit Tigers baseball team has the money to draft you for the minor leagues right out of high school? We're talking millions of dollars."

The teammates heard that, and they *all* began to dream.

Damion smiled and said, "Yeah, but that's in baseball."

Coach Bill smiled back at him through the rearview mirror. He said, "But once you have the money, Damion, and you know that your friend Taylor wants to make movies, then you can invest in his movies, and you both can become successful together. That's what I'm trying to teach you guys."

Damion and Taylor looked at each other in the back seat. Taylor smiled, but Damion shook his head.

"But what if I don't want to put my money into making his movies?" Damion asked.

"I know. His movies may not be any good," another one of their teammates suggested.

Those were the comments of rejection that Taylor was afraid of hearing from his teammates or anyone else. His smile quickly disappeared.

"You guys don't know that yet," Coach Bill challenged. "Taylor's a heck of a short stop. He swings a good bat. He runs the bases like a fox. He's a good student. He learns fast. He has a great attitude. He makes a lot of friends. He keeps everybody's attention. And I think he would make a great movie director one day. But if you guys wouldn't want to invest in him, then I guess you're right. Nobody around here has the money, because they're all afraid to put it on the line and do something different with it."

With that, all of the guys went silent, including Damion.

"But I'll tell you what, all of you guys can count on me to support you in any way that I can," Coach said. "And we need more people willing to step up and do all that they can."

"Yeah, Coach, you help us with everything," one of the teammates responded.

Coach Bill nodded and told them, "That's what it's all about, helping one another."

———

When they arrived back home in Detroit, Taylor was still energized from watching "Transformers."

"Hey, Taylor, how was the movies?" the younger kids on his block, including his younger sisters, asked him.

Coach Bill could hardly afford to take everyone. The baseball team was the group of guys he looked after.

Taylor said, "It was great! 'Transformers' was the best movie so far this summer."

The younger kids walked out on the front lawn of their housing complex to gather around him. "For real?" they asked. "I wish we could all go to see it," one of Taylor's younger sisters commented.

Once Taylor realized the kids had nothing to do and no Fourth of July fireworks, he immediately went into role playing with them.

"*The Transform-merrrs / more than meets the eyyyes . . .*" he sang to them before making transforming sound effects. He then started walking toward the kids like an evil robot.

"Where is my leader, Megatron?" he asked them in a deep, robotic voice.

The kids reacted by running away from him. They were smiling and laughing.

"You humans will tell me what I want *now*," he demanded, and he walked faster toward them. That made the younger kids run away faster and laugh harder. And when Taylor's sister fell down in front of him, he bent over and grabbed both of her arms to shake her body with imaginary shock waves.

"ZiiZiiZiiZiiZiiZiiZiiT!"

His sister broke out laughing on the ground.

Taylor said in his evil robot voice, "I will shock all of you humans until you tell me where I can find my leader, Megatron."

That made the kids even more excited. Some of the boys tried to attack Taylor's evil robot, while avoiding his shock waves.

"Get him! Get him!" they all yelled to each other, surrounding Taylor's evil robot in a circle.

Whenever any of the kids got too close, where he could grab them, Taylor shocked them into extreme laughter.

"ZiiZiiZiiZiiZiiZiiZiiT!"

Some of their parents watched him and laughed as well.

"That Taylor sure is something special with the kids," an adult commented from her front steps.

"Yeah, the kids love that boy," another parent agreed from her patio.

Damion walked out of his house with his baseball and glove in hand. He looked across the front lawn of their housing complex and immediately spotted his baseball teammate, chasing kids around while pretending to be a Transformer.

"That boy is crazy," he mumbled to himself. He thought that Taylor had lost his mind, so he shook his head and grinned.

But Taylor didn't see him. He was too busy having fun.

"ZiiZiiZiiZiiZiiZiiZiiT!"

Finally, Damion shouted, "Taylor, what are you doing, man?"

His excitable teammate looked back and answered, "I'm playing with the kids."

"Well, I need you to play catch with me," Damion told him with his glove and ball raised high.

Taylor stopped and stared at him for a minute. He asked Damion, "Why? The season is over with."

"Not for the *major* leagues," Damion responded. He wanted to start getting ready for his future early.

"We don't play in the major league," Taylor told him.

"Come on, man, are you gonna play catch with me or what? I want to practice my pitching."

Taylor started thinking that maybe the coach mentioning Damion as a major league draft choice had gone to the young pitcher's head. At the same time, Damion refused to support Taylor's movie dreams. Taylor figured, why should he help Damion out with his dreams of reaching baseball's major leagues by playing catch with him, if Damion would never support him?

So Taylor responded, "Not right now. I'm still playing with them."

"Yeah, but playing *what*?" Damion asked him. "Make-believe, monster robot? Come on, man. Let's play catch."

Taylor refused. "Nope. Not right now." And he went back to chasing the kids.

"ZiiZiiZiiZiiZiiZiiZiiT!"

Damion shook his head again and went to find someone else to catch his pitches. Taylor was too movie crazy.

Later on that night, some older teenagers and adults shot off Fourth of July fireworks while the neighborhood kids watched and shouted back and forth to one another.

"WOW! LOOK AT THAT ONE!"

"YEAH!"

"OOOOHH!"

"MAN, THAT WAS A BIG ONE!"

"DID YOU SEE THAT ONE?"

Although they were only a few feet apart, as they stood watching the fireworks with the rest of the neighborhood crowd at their housing complex, Damion and Taylor were still not speaking to one another. They both took their individual dreams seriously, and did not agree with the lack of support for each other.

"Hey, did you hear that Travis Brown was supposed to be shooting his video at the playground this weekend?" one of the teenage boys asked another. They were having conversations between the whistles, booms and bangs of the fireworks.

Travis Brown was a local Detroit rapper who had a recording deal with Warner Brothers Music. He had made his dream come true, and the neighborhood all supported him.

"Yeah, I heard about it, but I don't believe it," the other teenager responded. "I mean, why would he want to shoot a video at the playground? There's nothing fancy about our playground. That place is dirty."

Taylor overheard their conversation about a video shoot,

and he stuck his two cents in it. "Maybe Travis wants to show where he really grew up instead of some fancy house or boat party, because he grew up playing at the playground just like us," he added.

Both of the teenagers looked him over.

"Yeah, whatever. We'll see," replied the second teen. His doubts about the video shoot made Taylor think of Damion. And as soon as he looked in Damion's direction, he found that his teammate was staring right back at him.

Taylor was still hesitant to speak to Damion, but he forced himself to anyway. He had a great idea that could help both of their dreams.

"Did you hear them talking about Travis Brown's video shoot at our playground this weekend?" Taylor asked his teammate.

Damion was still mad at him for not wanting to play catch earlier. "Yeah, so what?" he answered with an attitude.

Taylor smiled and said, "You wanna show up in our uniforms and play catch and see if they'll put us in it?"

Damion paused. "Aw, man, you don't even know if they're gonna do it or not. They didn't announce it on the radio or anything."

"Maybe he doesn't want everybody to know," Taylor suggested. "They don't tell everybody when they're taping movies and commercials and stuff. There would be too many people in the way."

Damion thought about it. He said, "And what if nobody shows up?" he asked. "We'll be standing out there in our uniforms looking stupid."

"Well then, I'll just play catch with you in our uniforms. Is your uniform washed already?" Taylor asked him. He didn't want them to show up in dirty uniforms.

Damion frowned and said, "Of course, it's washed. My mom always washes my uniform. She even scrubs the grass stains out." Then he smiled from ear to ear. "She knows how clean I like it for the pitcher's mound," he said.

Taylor said, "Well, good. Let's do it then."

———

When Saturday morning came and Taylor knocked on Damion's door, bright and early, his teammate was fully dressed in his blue, red and white Red Sox uniform and was ready to go. He acted like it was the Little League Championship. Even his black and white cleats were shiny and clean. Damion was still unsure, however, if there was a video shoot that morning.

"I'm telling you, man, if there's no video, then you're gonna play catch with me as long as I want to for this," he said.

Taylor didn't care. They had no time to waste. He figured the video guys would set up their cameras early. So he said, "Okay, let's go."

Damion didn't budge. He said, "I'm serious, man. If there's no video, then you have to play catch for as long as I want."

"Okay, I'll do it," Taylor repeated. "Now let's go." He wanted to get to the playground as quickly as possible, so he started running.

"I'm not running there with you, man," Damion said. Everything was a push and pull game with him. But Taylor tricked him.

He smiled back and said, "I know you won't run, because you can't beat me."

The two of them had a base-running rivalry at practice and in the games. So Taylor's challenge got under Damion's skin.

"Whatever," he responded at first. But as Taylor continued to run, Damion got the idea that he could show just how fast he was by catching up to him from behind. He took off running like a kid on fire.

Once Taylor realized that his teammate was after him, he started to run faster, and they both reached the playground in a tie, three blocks away from where they lived.

"Now, boy, I tied you," Damion commented. "And you had a big head start on me."

Taylor looked forward and didn't care. He saw two big trucks at the playground with camera equipment everywhere.

"Look, look, look, I told you, I told you," he shouted, jumping up and down excitedly as they approached.

Damion looked forward and smiled. He was excited now himself. Then he frowned again. "But they still may not let us in it."

Taylor was determined to find out, so they approached the camera crew to look for a director.

There weren't that many people out there early. It was mostly the camera and lighting guys setting up the equipment. But as soon as the two boys got nearer, a tall, muscle man wearing all black appeared from nowhere to stop them.

"Hey kids, don't get too close over here."

"What are y'all doing?" Taylor asked him as if he didn't know.

The muscle man told him, "They're gonna be shooting a video later on." He didn't act too friendly about it either.

Taylor said, "For real? Who's the director?"

The muscle man shook his head and said, "Look now . . ."

Before he could get his words out, a slim, long-haired White guy, wearing a red designer T-shirt, blue jeans, and boots, looked over at them and asked, "Hey, you guys don't have a baseball game here today, do you?" He looked confused, staring at the two boys in their bright uniforms and ready baseball gloves.

Damion let Taylor do all of the talking. It was his idea, and like Coach Bill had said, Taylor was "Mr. Friendly."

"No, we don't have a game today. We were just looking for the director," Taylor told him.

The long-haired guy smiled. "You were looking for the director? For what?"

Taylor smiled and said, "We want to play catch in the video."

That's when Damion took the ball out of his glove.

The long-haired guy looked and started laughing. Then he challenged Taylor and Damion.

"Okay, are you guys any good?"

That was just what Taylor was hoping for. Damion was the best pitcher around, and Taylor had a great glove.

"Okay, let's show him your arm, Damion," Taylor said.

Damion grinned and backed up for space. He went into his pitcher's motion and hurled the ball straight at Taylor's opened glove.

POP!

It was a perfect throw with plenty of speed, and Taylor caught it like a major league pro.

The long-haired guy nodded his head and said, "That's good. Great arm, and nice catch," he told them both. "Well, I'll see what I can do for you guys about that director thing."

Taylor heard that and had to keep his cool. "Thanks!"

Then they noticed that the long-haired guy was telling everyone what to do.

"We need more light reflecting over here, and set up the dolly on this side," he told about five other guys.

Damion looked at Taylor and asked, "Isn't the director the one who tells everyone what they need to do?"

Taylor was still watching and wondering himself. He answered, "Yeah. I think it might be him," referring to the long-haired guy.

"Well, ask him again," Damion pressed Taylor. They were right next to him.

Taylor shook it off. "Not while he's busy," he commented. "He'll think we're bothering him. So we'll wait and start playing catch again after they have everything set up."

Damion looked at his teammate and grinned. "You're really into this movie thing."

Taylor smiled back and said, "And you're really into baseball."

"You play on the team," Damion told him. "You're good too."

"Yeah, but I want to make movies more than I want to play baseball," Taylor admitted. "I'm gonna play baseball for now because I still like it. And even when I do make movies, I'm still gonna be a baseball fan."

He grinned at his pitching teammate and told him, "And I'll still be watching you, playing for the Chicago Cubs or something."

Damion laughed and said, "You mean, the New York *Yankees*, boy."

"Whatever," Taylor commented.

However, when two hours had passed, and the long-haired guy had not looked in their direction again, Damion began to grow a little restless.

"Are you sure you want to keep on waiting without saying anything to him? Maybe he forgot about us."

Taylor continued to watch and wait as more people began to show up. Model girls walked into a costume and make-up trailer, fancy cars were being parked inside the camera angles, and curious community members began to come out, with more security stationed to keep them out of the way.

"Come on, man, what are you waiting for?" Damion pressed his friend.

Taylor was still studying everything. He had nearly forgotten that he wanted to be in the video. He started paying more attention to how they were setting up scenes. It was like a coach scouting a baseball team. Taylor was doing his movie-making homework. But Damion was not interested in that.

Finally, Taylor caught the director's eye again. He told him with a smile, "Don't forget about us," and that was it.

The director smiled back but said nothing.

"I don't know about this, man. He looks like he's just playing it off to me," Damion said.

"Chill, man, they haven't even started shooting anything yet. I'm not gonna let him forget about us," Taylor told him. "Come on, as much as I love movies and stuff. But I just know you can't bother him. He has to put this whole thing together."

"All right, if you say so," Damion mumbled.

After another hour, Travis Brown showed up with an entourage of 30 people, with more pretty girls included.

Taylor saw how much energy the rapper's arrival created, and he told his teammate, "Okay, they're about to get started now."

Damion had been ready to leave an hour before. "They *better* be ready," he said.

But once the star of the video arrived, the security went into overdrive and started moving everyone away from the set. It started to get really crowded.

"Aw, man, now we can't even get close to him. He can't see us playing ball way over here with all these people," Damion complained.

Taylor was concerned at that point himself. Maybe he had been too passive earlier.

"Hey, what are you guys doing out here in your uniforms?"

The boys turned and spotted Coach Bill in the crowd with them. And they were both happy to see him.

"Oh, hey, Coach Bill. We just wanted to get in the video and play catch with our uniforms on," Taylor explained.

Coach Bill chuckled and smiled. "That's a good idea."

"He came up with it himself," Damion admitted. "We even met the director before everybody came out here this morning. He saw me pitch and said we were both good. But now we can't even get close to him with all these people."

Coach Bill thought their dilemma over. "Did Travis get here yet? I used to coach his older brother, Terrance. And when Terrance got into trouble and ended up losing his life out in the streets, I continued to look out for Travis," Coach Bill told them.

"Aw, man, so you think you can talk to him about us getting in his video?" Taylor asked.

"I'll see what I can do," Coach Bill answered. "But I didn't know you guys wanted to be in a video. I could have asked him about it earlier."

"We didn't know he was even doing it until a couple days ago," Damion explained.

"And we didn't know that you knew him," Taylor added.

The coach nodded and took out his cell phone. "Yeah, I know him. And he didn't want too many people to know about this. Look at all the people out here now, and this is just from word of mouth."

Damion looked around at all the neighborhood supporters who filled the playground and said, "Yeah."

"Hey, what's up, Robby? This is Coach Bill Jackson," the coach said into his cell phone. Then he listened and grinned. "Yeah, I'm out here in this jam-packed crowd right now. But look here, man, I got two boys from my Red Sox team that almost made it to the citywide championship this summer, and I want them to meet Travis for inspiration. You know, they took it pretty bad when they lost in the playoffs a week ago."

Taylor and Damion looked at each other and grinned as their coach set up their chance meeting with the star rapper.

"Okay, so I'll step forward in the crowd with them then. They both have their Red Sox uniforms on."

When Coach Bill hung up his cell phone, he told his young players, "Now I didn't say anything about you guys being in the video. I'll let you two do that yourselves. I just wanted to get you in the room with him. I don't want it to seem like I'm trying to force him to do that. So you'll have to pitch that baseball idea yourself, Taylor. And then I'll back you up on it."

Damion smiled and said, "I thought I was the pitcher."

"Well, you told me it was Taylor's idea, right? So now it's his turn to pitch," the coach told his team leader. "A pitch is also a word that people use when they try to sell a creative business idea. And that's what this is," he said.

Damion nodded his head and said, "Oh." Then he looked at Taylor. "I guess it's all on you now, man. It's time to show and prove, like in baseball. You're up to the plate."

Taylor took a deep breath and smiled. "Okay," he uttered.

The three of them made their way through the crowd to reach the front, where the security men held everyone back and at a distance. Then Coach Bill waited there with his two eager players for Travis Brown's manager, Robby, to find them.

Robby, a thick-bodied, light brown man, wearing a white Detroit Tigers baseball cap, walked out from a video trailer and looked through the crowd. He was still holding his cell phone to his ear and talking.

"ROBBY!" Coach Bill yelled to him.

Robby turned to his left and spotted them. He told one of the security men to let them through.

Taylor and Damion followed behind their coach toward the video trailers where Travis Brown and his dancers were getting their outfits and make-up ready. They felt very special.

Damion looked over at Taylor and said, "Wow, this is cool."

Taylor smiled, but he was busy thinking about what he would say to Travis to get them in the video.

As soon as they walked into the small trailer behind Robby, they saw the long-haired director inside with Travis Brown and a few of the pretty girls. The director was explaining the video concept to them.

"So, we're going to shoot a number of scenes of you guys dancing and bobbing your heads to the music at various stations around the playground, while Travis raps," he was saying.

Travis looked bored as he listened. He was decked out in expensive blue jeans, platinum jewelry, and Detroit Tigers baseball gear. But when he saw Coach Bill walk in, he became excited. He even stood up from his chair to greet him.

"Hey, Coach B., what's going on? I was wondering if you were gonna make it out here today."

"Oh, yeah, I wasn't gonna miss this," Coach Bill told him as they shook hands and hugged.

The long-haired director looked annoyed after that. There were too many interruptions going on. But then he spotted the two boys he remembered from earlier and smiled.

"Hey guys," he said, and approached them.

Damion didn't have anything to say to him. The man had left them hanging outside in the crowd and had never come back to get them. But Taylor spoke up anyway.

"Did you forget about our baseball idea?" he asked. He said it loud enough for everyone inside the trailer to overhear. He figured he could reintroduce his video idea that way.

The director was surprised by it and stuttered. "Well, I, ah, or *we* had a lot of, ah, other things to prepare for on the shoot before I could get back to you guys. I mean, we have a lot of things to accomplish here today."

Travis looked over at the two teammates wearing their Red Sox baseball gear with their ready gloves in hand. He asked the coach, "Are these your guys?"

Robby, his manager, spoke up and answered, "Yeah, they wanted to meet you. Coach said they almost made the citywide championship this year."

Travis seemed interested. "Oh yeah, what was y'all record?"

Damion answered that question. "Twelve and two. And I was eight and one as the pitcher. But we lost the last playoff game by two runs. We had too many errors in the outfield."

Travis nodded and looked them over again. He saw that they were fully dressed for another game. "So, you have another game or something today?" he asked them, confused.

Damion looked at Taylor. It was his turn to answer with his pitch.

Taylor said, "No, we don't have another game. We just came out here to see your video and see if we can play catch in our uniforms in it. But we didn't know that Coach knew you."

Taylor's heart was beating fast. He didn't know if he was explaining things correctly or not. Was his first pitch a strike or a ball?

Then the long-haired director spoke up. "Yeah, these guys were out here bright and early this morning while we were still setting up. And they're good too. I think we could use them, you know, if we have the time for it."

All eyes were suddenly on Travis Brown. It was his decision. What would he say about it?

Taylor's heart was racing in his chest even faster now. *Please let us do it! Please let us do it! Please let us do it,* he begged in his mind.

One of the prettiest girls looked them over and said, "They're cute, Travis. Put them in the video. Go ahead and do it."

Travis looked at his manager, Robby.

Robby shrugged his shoulders. "I don't see nothing wrong with it. You know they can catch if Bill's coaching them."

Coach Bill finally spoke up with a nod and a smiled. "You're looking at two of my best players, my short stop and my pitcher."

"I can even drop the ball and have it hit me in the face because I'm watching a pretty girl's dance moves. That'll be funny," Taylor suggested.

They all looked at Taylor and laughed as if he were crazy.

"You want a baseball to hit you in the face?" Travis asked him.

"And then I can get a black eye and have the girl put ice on it for me," Taylor continued. "And kiss me on it."

They all laughed at him again. Even Damion laughed. Taylor was pressed.

Then the prettiest model said, "And that would be me that he's looking at."

"So, what do you want to be, a little actor or something?" Taylor sked him.

Taylor corrected him and said, "A director."

The long-haired director nodded to him. "I can see that. You're already thinking like a director. You're fast on your feet."

Travis Brown finally nodded. "Okay, we'll try something," he told them all. "But I don't know about you getting hit in the face with a baseball. And we definitely can't have you wearing those Boston Red Sox uniforms. So we gotta get you some Detroit Tigers gear that fits."

He looked at his manager. "Robby, call the assistants and have them run out and get us some Tigers' gear for kids."

Taylor and Damion started smiling from ear to ear.

By the time the camera crew had shot enough footage of the rap star, his pretty females dancers, his entourage of friends, and some of the extras who had shown up that morning, Taylor and Damion were dressed in brand new Detroit Tigers jerseys with baseball caps. They were ready to go.

"All right, are you guys ready for your scene?" the long-haired director asked them.

The boys both nodded and spaced out in front of each other to begin to play catch in front of the cameras, dancers, Travis Brown's guys, and all of the Detroit neighborhood spectators. Like Damion had said, it was just another game of catch, and with Coach Bill still there watching, the teammates looked like a couple of major league pros.

"That's good, that's good," the director told them. "Now let's have the first girl walk past and the throw ends up being a little high as your eyes roam in the wrong direction," he told Damion.

"And then I'll act mad that you overthrew me," Taylor said.

The director nodded to him and grinned. "Yeah, that's good. Action!"

The first pretty girl walked past while the boys played catch. Damion looked at her with wide eyes and threw the ball clearly over Taylor's head. Taylor jumped and extended his glove high to try and catch but missed.

"That's good, that's good," the director told them. "Now let's do a couple more of those."

Then Taylor snuck over to his teammate for a private discussion. "D., throw the ball right at my left eye, but don't throw it too hard. Okay?" he whispered.

Damion stared at him and whispered back, "But they said they didn't want you to do that."

"I know, I know, but do it anyway," Taylor argued. "They're gonna love it. Trust me. I know it."

"Okay, let's get another take," the director stated. "Action!"

The prettiest girl walked past Taylor, and he dropped his glove low and watched her with an open mouth as Damion threw the ball to him. Taylor saw the ball coming, but he didn't move until it hit him straight in his left eye. When it hit him, he jerked his head back and fell to the ground like a circus clown.

"Cheese and crackers!" the long-haired director shouted. He immediately ran over to see if the kid was all right. "Are you okay?" he asked Taylor.

Taylor leaned up and blinked with fresh tears running out of his eyes. "That was *perfect*." he said. "It stung a little bit, but I'm all right. Damion has the best aim around," he said.

They all walked over to watch the footage. And there it was. Taylor watches the pretty girl walk past him, he drops his glove low in front of his chest, Damion throws the baseball straight at him, but Taylor is staring at the girl. The ball smacks him straight in the eye and knocks him flat on his back.

Coach Bill shook his head and said, "Wow. You don't need another take of that. That *was* perfect."

Travis Brown laughed it off. "Yeah, now the boy's trying to steal my whole video. But we're definitely gonna use that. I can see people talking about it now, especially the kids."

When their part of the video shoot was over, Travis and Robby decided to pay the boys $200 apiece, and gave Coach

Bill release forms for their parents to sign. The forms would allow the production company to use the footage of the boys in the video.

Damion couldn't believe it. He counted the money five times inside the back of Coach Bill's SUV as he drove them home. "Man, this is the *awesome*," Damion stated.

Taylor was much more calm about it. "Now do you believe I can make money off of my movies?" he asked his friend.

Damion stopped, looked at him and nodded his head. "Taylor, if I ever make the major leagues, and you need some money to make your movies, then count me in, man. That's a promise, 'cause you *crazy*. You already got us in a video. *And* we got paid for it."

Coach Bill listened to the boys chat in the back seat as he drove them home. And he felt proud of them. They were learning that real teamwork is required to make big dreams come true.

ABOUT THE AUTHOR

Omar Tyree is a *New York Times* best-selling author whose 18 published books have sold nearly 2 million copies worldwide. A graduate of Howard University with a degree in Print Journalism, Tyree has been recognized as one of the most renowned contemporary writers in the African-American community. His contributions to literature have earned him a 2001 NAACP Image Award for Outstanding Literature in Fiction, and a 2006 Phillis Wheatley Literary Award for Body of Work in Urban Fiction. Tyree is also an informed and passionate speaker on various community-related topics.

A tireless creator, Tyree makes his children's book debut with *12 Brown Boys*, a collection of short stories for middle readers that focuses on the lives of Black pre-teen boys. "My goal is to turn urban boys on to reading, and then keep them reading by supplying them with more books with great content in the future."